The Haunting of Gravenhurst

Vivian Darkmoor

Contents

1. Prologue   1

2. Chapter 1   3

3. Chapter 2   9

4. Chapter 3   17

5. Chapter 4   26

6. Chapter 5   32

7. Chapter 6   38

8. Chapter 7   44

9. Chapter 8   49

10. Chapter 9   54

11. Chapter 10   59

12. Chapter 11   63

13. Chapter 12   68

14. Chapter 13   73

15. Chapter 14   78

16.	Chapter 15	84
17.	Chapter 16	88
18.	Chapter 17	92
19.	Chapter 18	96
20.	Chapter 19	100
21.	Chapter 20	104
22.	Chapter 21	109
23.	Chapter 22	115
24.	Chapter 23	122
25.	Chapter 24	128
26.	Chapter 25	133
27.	Chapter 26	139
28.	Chapter 27	145
29.	Chapter 28	151
30.	Chapter 29	155
31.	Chapter 30	160
32.	Chapter 31	164
33.	Chapter 32	170
34.	Chapter 33	174
35.	Epilogue	178

Prologue

In the quiet town of Eldridge, where every street corner holds a memory and every shadow whispers secrets, Gravenhurst Manor stands as an enigma shrouded in time and darkness. Once a grand estate, its walls have long since crumbled into decay, and its windows, now shattered and vacant, seem to watch over the town with a haunting vigilance.

Legend has it that the mansion was abandoned not by choice, but by necessity. Rumors speak of a night when the house itself seemed to come alive, its halls echoing with anguished cries and its rooms suffused with an otherworldly darkness. Those who lived through that night spoke of a malevolent presence that twisted reality, a force so powerful it drove them from their home and left them forever changed.

Decades later, the mansion's story has faded into a mere whisper of folklore, a tale told to thrill-seekers and ghost hunters who seek the thrill of the unknown. But for some, the call of the mansion is not easily ignored. It beckons with a voice as old as the shadows that cling to its walls, a voice that whispers of secrets yet to be uncovered.

Jade, Maya, Lena, and Carter are just ordinary high school students, their lives filled with the usual mix of dreams, fears, and teenage dilemmas. Yet, their paths are destined to cross with the mansion's dark legacy. Drawn by curiosity and a sense of adventure, they will soon discover that Gravenhurst Manor is not just a relic of the past, but a place where nightmares are born and reality is twisted beyond recognition.

As they step into the mansion's eerie embrace, they will face a darkness that defies comprehension. They will uncover truths that challenge their understanding of the world and themselves. And in the heart of the mansion, they will confront a force that has waited patiently for its moment to strike.

This is their story—a journey into the heart of darkness where every step takes them closer to the truth, and every shadow holds a piece of the past. It is a tale of bravery and fear, of friendship and betrayal, of a mansion that refuses to be forgotten.

Welcome to Gravenhurst Manor, where the past is never truly gone, and the shadows have a life of their own.

Chapter 1

I never wanted to come back here. My mother told me it would be a fresh start, a chance to move on from everything that happened. But all I could think about as we drove into town was how everything here felt like a whisper from the past—a ghostly echo that tugged at the edges of my mind. Maybe it was because of what happened last time we lived in a small town like this, or maybe it was just my curse to feel the weight of history in every place I visit. Either way, I knew this place wasn't going to be the clean slate my mom had promised.

My name is Lena Carter, and I can hear the past.

It's not like in the movies, where ghosts moan and rattle chains, or spirits appear in mirrors. It's more subtle than that, more like an old radio that picks up faint, static-filled signals. Sometimes it's a voice, sometimes a laugh or a scream. Other times it's just a feeling—a heavy sadness or a flash of anger that doesn't belong to me. It's always been like this for as long as I can remember, and I've never told anyone. Not even my mom.

We pulled into the driveway of our new house, a two-story colonial with peeling white paint and a sagging porch. It looked like something out of a horror movie, but my mom was all smiles as she got out of the car.

"Isn't it charming, Lena?" she asked, her voice too bright. "A little fixer-upper, but it's got character."

I nodded, forcing a smile. "Yeah, it's...quaint."

She ruffled my hair as she walked by, heading toward the front door with a bounce in her step. I envied her optimism, her ability to see only the good in every situation. She was always like that, even after Dad died. Especially after Dad died.

I grabbed my backpack from the car and slung it over my shoulder, feeling the familiar weight settle between my shoulder blades. It wasn't just schoolbooks in there—it was my sketchpad, my pencils, and a small journal I kept with me at all times. Drawing was the one thing that helped me focus, helped me block out the echoes.

As I followed my mom up the steps, I couldn't shake the feeling that the house was watching me. The windows were dark and empty, like eyes that had seen too much. I shivered, pulling my jacket tighter around me.

"Come on, Lena! I'll need your help unpacking," my mom called from inside.

I took a deep breath and stepped over the threshold. The air inside was musty, like the place hadn't been aired out in years. Dust motes floated in the sunlight streaming through the windows, and the wooden floors creaked under my weight. My mom was already bustling around, opening windows and humming to herself.

"Do you like your room?" she asked, pointing up the staircase. "It's the one with the bay window at the end of the hall."

I nodded, not trusting myself to speak. I headed upstairs, each step creaking louder than the last. The hallway was lined with old photographs, the kind that were black and white and slightly blurred, showing stern-looking people in old-fashioned clothes. Their eyes seemed to follow me as I passed by, and I quickened my pace.

My room was at the end of the hall, just like my mom said. The bay window overlooked the backyard, where a massive oak tree stood, its branches swaying gently in the breeze. The room was mostly empty, just a bed frame and a dresser left behind by the previous owners. But it was the window that caught my attention.

I walked over to it, placing my hand on the cool glass. The view outside was peaceful, almost serene. But as I stood there, I felt it—a faint whisper at the edge of my consciousness, like someone was standing right behind me, breathing softly in my ear.

"Help..."

I spun around, my heart racing, but the room was empty. Just the wind, I told myself. Just the wind and my overactive imagination. But deep down, I knew better.

I forced myself to breathe, to focus. I could control this—I had to. I pulled out my sketchpad and a pencil from my backpack and sat on the floor, leaning against the wall. Drawing always helped, even if it was just doodles. It was my way of grounding myself, of tuning out the echoes that threatened to overwhelm me.

As the pencil moved across the page, I felt the tension in my shoulders start to ease. I wasn't drawing anything specific, just letting my hand move freely, shapes and lines forming on their own. After a few minutes, I realized I was sketching the view from the window—the oak tree, the backyard, the faint outline of the old mansion in the distance.

The mansion. I hadn't noticed it before, but there it was, partially obscured by the trees. It looked abandoned, with ivy climbing up the stone walls and broken windows staring out like empty eye sockets. Something about it sent a shiver down my spine, but I couldn't look away.

"Lena? Are you okay up there?" my mom called from downstairs.

"Yeah, I'm fine," I called back, tearing my eyes away from the window. "Just unpacking."

I quickly shoved the sketchpad back into my backpack and stood up. I needed to get out of the house, to clear my head.

"Mom, I'm going to take a walk, okay?"

"Sure, honey! Just don't go too far, dinner will be ready soon."

I grabbed my jacket and headed out the door before she could say anything else. The cool air was a welcome relief after the stuffiness of the house, and I breathed it in deeply as I walked down the driveway.

The town was small, just a few streets lined with old houses and a main road that led to a handful of shops and a diner. It was the kind of place where everyone knew everyone else, where gossip spread faster than wildfire. I hated towns like this.

I kept walking, not really paying attention to where I was going, until I found myself standing in front of the old mansion. Up close, it was even more imposing, with its weathered stone walls and overgrown garden. The front gate was rusted and hanging off its hinges, and the path leading up to the front door was cracked and uneven.

For a moment, I considered turning back. But something about the mansion drew me in, like a magnet pulling me closer. I pushed open the gate, the metal groaning in protest, and stepped onto the path.

As I approached the front door, I heard it again—a faint whisper, just on the edge of hearing. It was like a voice calling out from the past, begging to be heard.

"Please..."

I froze, my heart pounding in my chest. The voice was clearer now, more desperate. I wanted to run, to get as far away from this place as possible, but my feet wouldn't move. It was like I was rooted to the spot, unable to tear myself away.

The door to the mansion was slightly ajar, and I could see darkness beyond it. The whispering grew louder, and I could feel it pressing in on me, like invisible hands trying to pull me inside.

"Lena..."

I stumbled back, my breath coming in short, panicked gasps. No. This wasn't happening. I wasn't going to let it happen. I turned and ran, not stopping until I was back at my house, my lungs burning and my legs shaking.

I slammed the front door behind me and leaned against it, trying to catch my breath. My mom appeared in the hallway, concern etched on her face.

"Lena, what's wrong? You look like you've seen a ghost."

I forced a laugh, shaking my head. "I'm fine, Mom. Just...out of shape, I guess."

She didn't look convinced, but she didn't press the issue. "Okay. Well, dinner's almost ready. Why don't you wash up and come help me set the table?"

I nodded, grateful for the distraction. As I headed to the bathroom, I caught a glimpse of myself in the mirror. My face was pale, my eyes wide and frightened. I splashed cold water on my face, trying to shake off the lingering feeling of dread.

But no matter how hard I tried, I couldn't forget the voice I'd heard at the mansion.

"Lena..."

It had called my name. And deep down, I knew that whatever was waiting in that mansion wasn't going to let me go so easily.

Chapter 2

The next morning, the sky was a dull gray, clouds hanging low like a heavy blanket. It suited my mood perfectly. I barely slept last night, tossing and turning as the memory of that voice played on repeat in my head. I tried convincing myself it was just my imagination, a product of stress from the move, but deep down, I knew better.

By the time my alarm went off, I felt like I hadn't slept at all. I dragged myself out of bed and went through the motions-brushing my teeth, pulling on my clothes, and stuffing my sketchpad into my backpack. I caught a glimpse of the mansion drawing I'd made the day before. The lines were sharp, almost angry, with dark shadows looming over the structure. I shoved the pad deeper into my bag, trying to forget about it.

When I got downstairs, my mom was already in the kitchen, humming as she made breakfast. She greeted me with a smile that was too bright for such an early hour.

"Good morning, sweetie! How did you sleep?"

"Fine," I lied, grabbing a piece of toast. "Thanks."

"Do you want a ride to school today?"

I shook my head. "I'll walk. It's not far, right?"

"No, just a few blocks," she said, her voice tinged with worry. "Are you sure? It's your first day, and I don't mind-"

"I'm sure," I cut her off, not wanting to prolong the conversation. The last thing I needed was my mom hovering over me at school.

She nodded, though I could see the concern in her eyes. "Alright. But if you need anything, just call me, okay?"

"Okay," I muttered, finishing my toast. I grabbed my bag and headed for the door before she could say anything else.

The walk to school was short, just like my mom said, but it felt like it took forever. The streets were mostly empty, save for a few kids my age walking in groups, talking and laughing. I kept my head down, not wanting to draw attention to myself. I was the new girl, the outsider, and I had no interest in making a scene on my first day.

When I finally reached the school, a sprawling brick building with ivy creeping up the sides, my stomach twisted with nerves. I hated first days. The awkward introductions, the curious stares, the inevitable questions about where I was from and why I'd moved here. It was all so exhausting.

I took a deep breath and walked through the front doors, clutching my schedule in one hand. The hallways were bustling with students, everyone chattering and shoving books into lockers. I found mine quickly enough-locker 347, right in the middle of a long row. I twisted the combination lock a few times before it clicked open, and I shoved my bag inside.

"Hey, you must be new."

I jumped at the sound of a voice beside me. A tall girl with long, dark hair and sharp eyes was leaning against the locker next to mine, her arms crossed. She had a confident air about her, like she'd been at this school forever and knew everything there was to know.

"Uh, yeah," I stammered. "I'm Lena."

"Jade," she said, her eyes raking over me like she was sizing me up. "Where are you from?"

"Uh...all over," I said, feeling my cheeks flush. "We move around a lot."

"Military?"

"No, just...family stuff," I mumbled, not wanting to get into it.

Jade shrugged, apparently satisfied with my answer. "Well, welcome to the middle of nowhere. Hope you like small towns."

I forced a smile. "Yeah, thanks."

She gave me a look, one eyebrow raised like she was trying to figure me out. Before she could ask anything else, the bell rang, and she pushed off the locker with a grin. "Better get to class. See you around, new girl."

I watched her disappear into the crowd, feeling a strange mix of relief and curiosity. Jade was intense, but there was something about her that intrigued me. I shook my head, pushing the thought aside, and grabbed my schedule. My first class was English, room 214.

As I made my way through the halls, I tried to keep a low profile, slipping into the classroom just as the final bell rang. The teacher, a middle-aged woman with glasses perched on the edge of her nose, glanced up as I entered.

"You must be Lena Carter," she said, her voice flat. "Welcome. Take a seat anywhere."

I nodded and slid into an empty desk near the back, avoiding the curious glances from the other students. The teacher, Mrs.

Reynolds, launched into a lecture about the reading list for the semester, and I did my best to focus, but my mind kept wandering back to the mansion, to the voice I'd heard.

It wasn't until Mrs. Reynolds mentioned a group project that I snapped back to attention.

"You'll be working in pairs for this assignment," she was saying, "researching a historical event from our town and presenting your findings. You can choose your partner, but remember, this is worth a significant portion of your grade."

The class buzzed with excitement as everyone started pairing up. I bit my lip, feeling a wave of anxiety wash over me. I didn't know anyone here. Who was I supposed to-

"Hey, new girl."

I looked up to see Jade standing over my desk, a smirk on her face. "Need a partner?"

"Uh, sure," I said, relieved that I didn't have to awkwardly ask someone. "Thanks."

"No problem," she said, sliding into the seat next to me. "This project's going to be a breeze."

As the noise in the classroom died down, Mrs. Reynolds continued. "Once you've chosen your partner, you'll need to select a topic. The town library has a section dedicated to local history. I suggest you start there."

Jade leaned over, her voice low. "You know, there's a lot of weird history in this town. We should pick something interesting."

"Like what?" I asked, curious.

She shrugged. "There's that old mansion on the outskirts of town. Rumor has it something creepy happened there years ago. Maybe we could dig into that?"

My heart skipped a beat. The mansion. The same one that had haunted my thoughts all night. I hesitated, not sure if I wanted to get any closer to whatever was lurking in that place. But Jade was watching me, waiting for an answer.

"Yeah," I said finally. "That sounds...interesting."

Jade grinned. "Awesome. We can head to the library after school and see what we can find."

I nodded, my stomach twisting with a mix of fear and anticipation. Maybe this project would help me figure out what was going on with the mansion-and with me.

The rest of the day passed in a blur of new faces and unfamiliar classrooms. I kept my head down, taking notes and trying to avoid too much attention. It wasn't until lunch that I realized how alone I felt. I stood in the cafeteria, tray in hand, scanning the room for a familiar face. But of course, there wasn't one.

"Lena! Over here!"

I turned to see Jade waving me over to a table near the windows. She was sitting with two other people-one was a tall, muscular guy with messy brown hair, the other a petite girl with glasses and a shy smile.

I hesitated, then walked over, grateful for the invitation.

"This is Lena," Jade said as I sat down. "Lena, meet Ethan and Maya."

"Hi," I said, offering a small smile.

Ethan nodded in acknowledgment, his attention more on his food than on me. Maya, on the other hand, smiled warmly.

"Nice to meet you, Lena. Jade told us you're new."

"Yeah," I said, picking at my food. "Just moved here."

"Where from?" Ethan asked, his voice deep and slightly disinterested.

"Here and there," I said vaguely, not wanting to go into details.

Jade rolled her eyes. "Come on, Ethan, don't interrogate her. She's new, give her a break."

Ethan shrugged. "Just making conversation."

"So, Lena and I are doing the history project together," Jade said, steering the conversation back on track. "We're going to research the old mansion."

Maya's eyes widened. "The mansion? That place is creepy."

"Exactly," Jade said with a grin. "That's what makes it interesting."

Ethan finally looked up, his expression curious. "You're talking about the Mason House, right? The one on the edge of town?"

"Yeah," I said, feeling a chill at the mention of the name.

Ethan frowned. "There's a lot of stories about that place. Most of them aren't good."

Jade waved a hand dismissively. "That's what makes it the perfect topic. We can separate fact from fiction, find out what really happened there."

Maya bit her lip, looking nervous. "Just...be careful, okay? My grandma used to tell me stories about that house. She said it's cursed."

Jade laughed. "Cursed? Come on, Maya. It's just an old house."

Maya didn't look convinced, but she didn't argue. I stayed quiet, my thoughts racing. The more I learned about this place, the more uneasy I felt. But at the same time, I was drawn to it, like a moth to a flame.

After school, Jade and I headed to the town library. It was an old building, with towering shelves and a musty smell that made me think of forgotten things. The librarian, an elderly woman with a stern expression, directed us to the section on local history. Jade immediately started pulling books off the shelves, flipping through them with an eagerness that surprised me.

"This place is a goldmine," she said, her eyes gleaming as she skimmed through the pages. "There's so much weird stuff about this town."

I picked up a book titled *Mysterious Happenings in Stonebrook*, the town's name etched in faded gold letters on the cover. Flipping through it, I found a chapter dedicated to the Mason House. The pages were yellowed with age, the text recounting various stories about the mansion-hauntings, disappearances, and unexplained phenomena.

"Listen to this," I said, my voice hushed. "In the late 1800s, a girl named Eliza Mason disappeared from the mansion without a trace. They searched for her for weeks, but she was never found. Some say she ran away, others think something...darker happened."

Jade leaned over to read, her expression serious. "Eliza Mason... I've heard that name before. They say her ghost still haunts the mansion, looking for revenge."

"Revenge for what?" I asked, feeling a shiver run down my spine.

"No one really knows," Jade said, sitting back in her chair. "Some say she was murdered by someone close to her. Others think it was an accident and that she's just lost. Either way, her spirit's supposed to be restless."

I stared at the page, my mind racing. The voice I heard at the mansion... could it have been Eliza? Was she trying to reach out to me? The thought made my heart race with a mix of fear and curiosity.

"We should look into this," Jade said, her voice tinged with excitement. "If we can uncover what really happened to Eliza, it could be a huge deal. We might even be able to set her spirit free."

The idea of investigating the mansion both terrified and intrigued me. Part of me wanted to run as far away as possible, but another part of me-the part that had always been drawn to the mysteries of the past-wanted to know more.

"Okay," I said finally. "Let's do it."

Jade grinned, her eyes sparkling with excitement. "This is going to be epic."

As we gathered our notes and headed out of the library, I couldn't shake the feeling that we were about to uncover something far more dangerous than we bargained for. But it was too late to turn back now. The echoes of the past were calling to me, and I knew I had to follow them, no matter where they led.

Chapter 3

The wind howled outside my window that night, rattling the old glass panes and making the tree branches scrape against the house like bony fingers. I couldn't sleep, not after what I'd read about Eliza Mason. Her name echoed in my mind, mingling with the voice I'd heard at the mansion. I knew it had to be her. It made too much sense, even if the thought scared me more than I wanted to admit.

I tossed and turned, the sheets tangling around my legs as I tried to get comfortable. But every time I closed my eyes, I saw the mansion, dark and looming, with the shadows pressing in on all sides. And I heard her—soft at first, then louder, more insistent.

"Lena…"

I sat bolt upright in bed, my heart pounding. The voice was clearer now, almost as if it were coming from right beside me. I scanned the room, but of course, it was empty. Just the wind, I told myself again, even though I knew it wasn't true.

With a shaky breath, I grabbed my sketchpad from the nightstand and flipped it open. Drawing always helped to calm me down, to make sense of the chaos in my mind. I let the pencil move across the page, not really thinking about what I was drawing, just letting my hand guide me.

Slowly, an image began to form—dark lines that twisted and turned into the outline of the mansion. The windows stared out like hollow eyes, and the front door was slightly ajar, as if inviting me in. But what drew my attention was the figure standing in the doorway. It was a girl, her features blurred, but her eyes sharp and full of sorrow.

"Eliza," I whispered, my hand freezing mid-stroke. I could feel her now, like a cold breeze brushing against my skin. She was here, in the room with me, or at least a part of her was.

"Help me..."

The voice was so clear, so desperate, that it sent a jolt of fear through me. My pencil slipped from my fingers, rolling off the bed and clattering to the floor. I stared at the drawing, at the girl's sorrowful eyes, and felt a lump form in my throat.

I didn't know what she wanted, or how I was supposed to help her, but I knew I couldn't ignore it. Not anymore.

The next morning, I was up before the sun, dark circles under my eyes and my nerves frayed from lack of sleep. My mom noticed as soon as I stumbled into the kitchen.

"Lena, you look exhausted," she said, her voice full of concern. "Are you feeling okay?"

"I'm fine," I muttered, grabbing a piece of toast. "Just didn't sleep well."

She frowned, clearly not convinced. "Are you sure? Maybe you should stay home today, get some rest."

"I'm fine," I repeated, more forcefully this time. "I just... I have a lot on my mind."

She studied me for a moment, then sighed. "Okay, but if you're not feeling well later, call me, alright?"

"Alright," I said, though I had no intention of doing so. The last thing I needed was my mom fussing over me when I was trying to figure out what was happening with Eliza.

By the time I got to school, the hallways were already buzzing with energy. I felt like a zombie as I made my way to my locker, my mind still stuck on the voice, on Eliza's sorrowful eyes.

"Lena! Over here!"

I looked up to see Jade waving me over, her usual grin plastered on her face. Ethan and Maya were with her, both of them looking a little more serious.

"Hey," I said, trying to muster up some enthusiasm.

Jade raised an eyebrow. "You look like you didn't sleep at all. Did you stay up late working on our project or something?"

"Or something," I muttered, leaning against the locker.

Maya frowned, her eyes full of concern. "You do look really tired, Lena. Are you okay?"

"Yeah, I'm fine," I said quickly, not wanting to get into it. "Just a rough night."

Ethan gave me a skeptical look but didn't press the issue. Instead, he changed the subject. "So, what's the plan? Are we heading back to the library today?"

"Actually," I said, my voice hesitant, "I was thinking... maybe we should go to the mansion."

Jade's eyes lit up. "Yes! I've been dying to check that place out. I didn't think you'd be up for it, though. I mean, you seemed kind of freaked out yesterday."

"I was," I admitted, "but I think... I think there's something we need to see there. Something important."

Maya looked uneasy, glancing between Jade and me. "I don't know, guys. The mansion gives me the creeps."

"It'll be fine," Jade said, brushing off her concerns. "We'll go after school, just for a quick look around. It's not like we're going to spend the night there or anything."

"Yeah, just a quick look," I agreed, though my stomach churned at the thought of going back. But I couldn't shake the feeling that Eliza was trying to show me something, and I needed to figure out what it was.

Ethan nodded, clearly intrigued. "Alright, I'm in. We should be careful, though. That place is old, and who knows what kind of condition it's in."

"Agreed," Jade said, her grin widening. "This is going to be awesome."

Maya still looked nervous, but she eventually nodded. "Okay, but let's be quick. I don't want to be there after dark."

After school, we all met up in the parking lot, the excitement and tension in the air palpable. Jade was practically bouncing with energy, while Maya clutched her backpack like it was a lifeline. Ethan was his usual calm self, though I could see a flicker of curiosity in his eyes.

"Ready?" Jade asked, looking around at us.

"Yeah," I said, my voice steady despite the anxiety gnawing at my insides.

The walk to the mansion was shorter than I remembered, or maybe it just felt that way because I was so focused on what we were about to do. The old gate creaked as we pushed it open, and the path leading up to the front door was overgrown with weeds. The mansion loomed ahead, even more imposing in the gray afternoon light.

"Wow," Ethan muttered, taking in the sight of the crumbling stone walls and broken windows. "This place is even creepier up close."

Jade grinned. "Told you it was awesome."

Maya shivered, glancing around nervously. "Let's just hurry up and get this over with."

We approached the front door, which was still slightly ajar, just like in my drawing. I hesitated, feeling a cold dread settle in my chest. I could almost hear the whispers again, faint but growing louder the closer we got.

"Lena?" Jade's voice snapped me out of my thoughts. "You okay?"

"Yeah," I said, forcing myself to take a step forward. "I'm fine. Let's go."

With a deep breath, I pushed the door open the rest of the way. It groaned on its hinges, the sound echoing through the dark, empty halls beyond. The air inside was cold, and the smell of mildew and decay hit me like a wave. The interior was just as I remembered—dusty, dark, and filled with shadows that seemed to move just out of the corner of my eye.

"Creepy," Jade whispered, her voice full of awe.

"Let's make this quick," Ethan said, his voice low. "We don't know how stable this place is."

We stepped inside, the floorboards creaking under our weight. The mansion was eerily quiet, the only sound the faint rustling of the wind outside. I couldn't shake the feeling that we were being watched, that something was lurking just beyond the shadows.

"Where do we start?" Maya asked, her voice trembling slightly.

"The main hall, I guess," I said, though I wasn't entirely sure. I was going off instinct, following the faint tug of something deep inside me.

We moved deeper into the mansion, the air growing colder with each step. The walls were lined with old portraits, their faces blurred with age and dust. It felt like they were watching us, their eyes following our every move.

"Lena, look at this," Jade said, stopping in front of a large painting. It depicted a young girl in a white dress, her dark hair cascading over her shoulders. She was standing in front of the mansion, her expression serene yet sad.

"Eliza Mason," I whispered, recognizing the name from the book.

"She was beautiful," Maya said softly, her eyes fixed on the portrait.

"Yeah," Jade agreed. "But there's something... off about her. I can't put my finger on it."

I stared at the painting, feeling a strange connection to the girl in the portrait. It was like she was staring back at me, her eyes full of secrets she couldn't share.

"Lena?"

The voice was so soft, so faint, that I almost didn't hear it. But it was there, just at the edge of my consciousness, pulling me further into the mansion.

"This way," I said, not even sure where I was going. I just knew I had to follow the voice, had to find out what Eliza was trying to tell me.

We moved deeper into the mansion, the creaking of the floor-boards and the faint echoes of our footsteps the only sounds. The voice—Eliza's voice—seemed to guide me, pulling me towards the heart of the house.

We reached a large wooden door at the end of the hall. It was different from the others, newer, as if it had been replaced recently. My hand hesitated on the handle, my heart pounding in my chest.

"This must be it," I said quietly. I could feel the others behind me, their tension mirroring my own.

"Are you sure about this?" Ethan asked, his voice low.

I nodded, though I wasn't sure of anything anymore. I just knew I had to open that door. With a deep breath, I turned the handle and pushed it open.

The room beyond was small and dark, the only light coming from a narrow window on the far wall. Dust motes floated in the air, disturbed by our presence. But what caught my attention was the object in the center of the room—a large, old-fashioned trunk, its surface covered in a thick layer of dust.

"Why would a trunk be locked away in a room like this?" Jade wondered aloud, her curiosity piqued.

"I don't know," I admitted, stepping closer to the trunk. I could feel a strange energy emanating from it, almost like it was alive. My fingers brushed against the latch, and I hesitated, a deep sense of foreboding settling over me.

"Lena…" Eliza's voice was clearer now, more desperate. She was here, right beside me. I could almost feel her cold presence in the air. "Please…"

"Lena?" Maya's voice brought me back to the present. She was watching me with wide, anxious eyes.

"I have to open it," I said, though I wasn't sure why. It felt like I had no choice, like this was what Eliza had been leading me to all along.

With trembling hands, I unlatched the trunk and slowly lifted the lid. The hinges creaked, the sound echoing in the small room. Inside, the trunk was filled with old, tattered clothes, letters, and a small, ornate box.

"What is all this?" Ethan asked, leaning in to get a better look.

"These must be Eliza's things," I whispered, reaching for the box. It was made of dark wood, intricately carved with floral patterns. My fingers brushed over the surface, and I felt a shock of cold run through me.

"Careful," Jade warned, though her eyes were locked on the box, just as intrigued as I was.

I opened the box slowly, revealing a delicate silver locket nestled inside. It was beautiful, the metal gleaming even in the dim light. But there was something about it that felt… wrong. As soon as I touched it, a wave of sorrow and fear washed over me.

"This must have been Eliza's," Maya said softly, her voice filled with sympathy.

"I think so," I agreed, though I was struggling to breathe. The emotions radiating from the locket were overwhelming, almost suffocating.

"Lena… help me…"

Eliza's voice echoed in my mind, clearer and more urgent than ever. I felt tears sting my eyes as the weight of her despair crashed over me.

"We have to find out what happened to her," I said, my voice trembling. "We have to help her."

Jade nodded, her expression serious for once. "We will. We'll figure this out together."

But as I looked at the locket in my hand, I couldn't shake the feeling that we were in over our heads. Whatever had happened to Eliza, it was something dark, something that had left a stain on this place—and on her.

And now, it was pulling us in too.

Chapter 4

The next few days were a blur of anxiety and unanswered questions. Every time I tried to focus on schoolwork or even just hang out with my friends, my mind kept drifting back to the mansion, to Eliza, and to that locket. I kept it hidden in my room, tucked away in the back of my desk drawer, but I could feel its presence, like it was calling out to me.

The others were just as affected. Jade, usually the life of the group, had grown quiet and contemplative, spending hours in the library researching the mansion and Eliza's past. Maya, on the other hand, seemed jumpy, constantly looking over her shoulder like she was expecting something-or someone-to appear out of thin air. Even Ethan, who was usually calm and logical, was clearly troubled, his brow furrowed with concern whenever the mansion came up.

We all knew that we had uncovered something bigger than we could have imagined, but none of us knew what to do next. We were just a bunch of high school kids poking around in things we didn't understand. But one thing was clear: we couldn't stop now. Eliza's voice haunted my dreams, her plea for help echoing in my ears even when I was awake.

It was Friday afternoon, and we had gathered at Jade's house to discuss our next steps. Her room was filled with books, papers, and notes she'd been compiling, and the air was thick with the scent of old paper and ink. Jade sat cross-legged on her bed, her laptop open in front of her, while Ethan and Maya were on the floor, surrounded by stacks of books.

"I found something," Jade announced, breaking the heavy silence. "It's about the Mason family."

"What is it?" I asked, leaning forward in my chair. My heart was pounding, a mix of fear and anticipation.

Jade's eyes flicked to me before she continued. "The Masons were one of the wealthiest families in Stonebrook back in the 1800s. They owned a lot of land and had a reputation for being... well, let's just say, not the most pleasant people. There were rumors about them, about strange things happening at the mansion."

"Like what?" Maya asked, her voice barely above a whisper.

Jade hesitated, then pulled up a document on her laptop. "I found some old newspaper clippings and diary entries from people who lived in the town back then. There were stories about disappearances-people who worked at the mansion just... vanishing. And then there's this." She turned the laptop towards us, showing us a scanned page from an old journal.

It was written in elegant, looping script, but the words themselves sent a chill down my spine.

I fear for the safety of my family. The Masons are not to be trusted. There is something evil in that house, something that preys on the souls of those who enter. I have heard the cries in the night, the whispers that speak of darkness and despair. May God protect us all.

The entry was dated 1892, the year Eliza disappeared.

"So, what are you saying?" Ethan asked, his voice tense. "That the Masons were involved in something supernatural?"

Jade shook her head. "I don't know. But whatever it was, it wasn't good. And I think it had something to do with Eliza."

A heavy silence fell over the room as we all absorbed the information. It felt like the air had grown colder, the shadows in the corners of the room deeper.

"What do we do now?" Maya asked, hugging her knees to her chest.

"I think we need to go back," I said, my voice trembling slightly. "There's more to this, something we're missing. I keep hearing her voice, asking for help. She's trying to tell us something."

Jade nodded slowly. "I agree. But we need to be careful. Whatever happened to Eliza, it wasn't just an accident. There's something evil in that mansion, and we need to be prepared."

"How do we prepare for something like this?" Ethan asked, a hint of skepticism in his voice. "It's not like we can just walk in there with a flashlight and hope for the best."

"We need to learn more," Jade said firmly. "There has to be something in these books, something that can help us. And maybe we should bring someone else in-someone who knows about this kind of stuff."

"Like who?" Maya asked, her voice tinged with fear.

"I don't know, maybe a historian or... a paranormal investigator?" Jade suggested, though she didn't sound entirely confident.

The idea of involving someone else made me uneasy. What if they didn't believe us? What if they thought we were just a bunch of kids with overactive imaginations? But at the same time, we were clearly out of our depth.

"Maybe we could ask Mr. Whitaker," I said suddenly. Mr. Whitaker was our history teacher, a gruff, no-nonsense man who had a reputation for knowing everything there was to know about Stonebrook's past. He was also the advisor for the school's history club, which Jade and I were both part of.

Jade's eyes lit up. "That's a great idea! Mr. Whitaker knows more about this town than anyone. If anyone can help us, it's him."

"I don't know," Ethan said, frowning. "What if he thinks we're crazy?"

"He won't," I said, though I wasn't entirely sure. "Mr. Whitaker loves this kind of stuff. If we show him what we've found, he'll take us seriously."

Maya still looked doubtful, but she didn't argue. "Okay, but we need to be careful. I don't want to mess with something we don't understand."

"Agreed," Jade said, closing her laptop. "Let's meet up after school on Monday and talk to Mr. Whitaker. In the meantime, we should all do some more research. There has to be something we're missing."

The meeting broke up soon after that, everyone leaving with a heavy sense of unease. As I walked home, the sun setting behind me, I couldn't shake the feeling that we were being watched. I kept glancing over my shoulder, but the streets were empty, the shadows growing longer with each passing minute.

When I finally reached my house, I felt a wave of relief. But as soon as I stepped inside, the atmosphere felt different-heavier, almost oppressive. I brushed it off as paranoia, trying to focus on anything but the mansion, but it was impossible. Eliza's voice was in my head, echoing in the silence of the house.

That night, I had the same dream. I was in the mansion, walking down the dark hallways, my footsteps echoing off the walls. The air was thick with dust, and the shadows seemed to stretch and twist in unnatural ways. I could hear the faint sound of crying, and I knew it was Eliza. I followed the sound, my heart pounding, until I reached the same wooden door.

When I opened it, the room was empty except for the trunk in the center. But this time, the trunk was open, and the locket was floating above it, glowing with a cold, silver light. As I stepped closer, the light grew brighter, until it was almost blinding.

"Lena..."

Her voice was so close now, so clear. I could feel her sadness, her fear, and something else-something darker, something that sent a chill down my spine.

Suddenly, the light exploded, and I was thrown backwards. I landed hard on the floor, the breath knocked out of me. When I looked up, I saw a figure standing in the doorway-a tall, dark figure, its face obscured by shadows. It radiated a malevolent energy, and I could feel its gaze on me, cold and piercing.

"Leave..."

The voice was deep and guttural, and it reverberated through my bones. I tried to move, to get up and run, but I was frozen in place, paralyzed by fear.

The figure stepped closer, its presence overwhelming, suffocating. I could feel the darkness closing in, choking me, and I knew I had to get out, had to escape.

With a scream, I forced myself to wake up, bolting upright in bed. My heart was racing, my body drenched in sweat. I could still feel the weight of that malevolent presence, still hear its voice echoing in my mind.

For a long time, I just sat there, trembling, trying to convince myself it was just a dream. But deep down, I knew it wasn't. Eliza wasn't the only one trapped in that mansion. There was something else-something dangerous, something that didn't want us there.

And it wasn't going to let us leave without a fight.

Chapter 5

Monday came faster than I had hoped. The weekend was a restless one, filled with dreams of dark hallways and looming shadows. Every time I closed my eyes, I saw the menacing figure from my nightmare, and the weight of the mansion's curse felt heavier.

At school, the tension was palpable among our group. Jade, Maya, and Ethan met me before class, their faces reflecting the same worry I felt. We exchanged glances, our silent understanding of the gravity of our situation hanging in the air.

"Are we really going to talk to Mr. Whitaker today?" Maya asked as we walked down the hall to history class.

"I think we have to," I replied. "We need answers, and he might be the only one who can help us."

"Let's hope he doesn't think we're just making this up," Ethan said, his brow furrowed. "If he does, we might be in for a rough ride."

The bell rang, signaling the start of first period. We filed into Mr. Whitaker's classroom, trying to appear casual despite our nerves. The room was its usual organized chaos, with maps, historical artifacts, and old books lining the shelves. Mr. Whitaker stood at the front, his stern expression softening as he noticed us.

"Ah, the history club," he said, his tone a mix of curiosity and mild surprise. "What brings you here this early?"

"We have something important to discuss," Jade said, stepping forward. "It's about the Mason mansion."

Mr. Whitaker's interest was piqued immediately. He gestured for us to sit. "The Mason mansion, you say? I've heard a few things about it. What's going on?"

We explained our findings-the locket, the diary entry, and our experiences in the mansion. As we spoke, Mr. Whitaker's expression shifted from skepticism to concern. When we finished, he leaned back in his chair, deep in thought.

"This is quite serious," he finally said. "I've studied the Masons' history in passing, but I didn't realize there were supernatural elements involved. There were rumors, yes, but nothing concrete."

"Can you help us?" I asked, my voice tinged with desperation.

"I can try," he replied. "But we need to be thorough. There's a lot of history to untangle, and we might need additional resources. I suggest we start by reviewing any archives and documents related to the Mason family and the mansion's history."

Jade's eyes lit up. "We've already started researching, but we could use more guidance."

"Good," Mr. Whitaker said. "I'll help you get access to some of the town's historical records. In the meantime, be careful. It sounds like there's more to this than meets the eye. And if you experience anything unusual, let me know immediately."

"Thank you, Mr. Whitaker," I said, feeling a bit of relief. "We'll keep you updated."

With our meeting concluded, Mr. Whitaker gave us access to a small archive room in the library where we could examine old records and documents. We spent the rest of the day poring over yellowed newspapers and brittle diaries, searching for any clue that might explain the mansion's dark history.

As we sifted through documents, we discovered more disturbing accounts. One diary entry described strange rituals performed by the Masons, and old newspapers mentioned unexplained disappearances. But the most chilling find was a letter detailing a curse placed upon the mansion by a rival family.

The letter was from a man named Jonathan Rook, who had a personal vendetta against the Masons. It spoke of a ritual meant to bind the souls of the Masons to the mansion, ensuring that they would suffer for their wrongdoings.

"This sounds like it could be related to Eliza's story," Ethan said, reading over my shoulder. "If the Masons were cursed, it might explain why Eliza's spirit is trapped there."

"Possibly," Jade said, scanning another document. "But we still don't know exactly how the curse works or what it means for us."

"I think we should go back to the mansion," Maya said suddenly. "There's got to be something there we missed."

I hesitated. "It's risky. We barely made it out last time."

"But we need more information," Maya insisted. "If we want to help Eliza and figure out what's really going on, we have to take the risk."

Jade nodded in agreement. "Maya's right. We need to be prepared, though. We should bring equipment-flashlights, cameras, and maybe even some protective symbols."

Over the next few days, we prepared for our return to the mansion. Jade found some old symbols used in protection rituals, and we gathered equipment to document our findings. Each of us was on edge, aware of the potential dangers but driven by the need to uncover the truth.

When Friday evening arrived, we met at the edge of the mansion's property. The sun was setting, casting long shadows over the overgrown lawn. The mansion loomed ahead, its silhouette dark and foreboding against the twilight sky.

"Ready?" Ethan asked, his voice steady but his eyes betraying his anxiety.

"As ready as we'll ever be," I replied, trying to sound confident.

We made our way to the front door, the old wood creaking under our weight. The mansion's interior was as unsettling as ever, the air thick with dust and the scent of decay. We moved cautiously, our flashlights cutting through the darkness.

We started with the room where we had found the locket. The trunk was still there, but now it was closed, as if someone had been tampering with it. I approached it carefully, my heart racing. When I opened it, the locket was gone.

"It's not here," I said, trying to keep my voice steady.

"Maybe someone took it,' Jade suggested, though her tone was uncertain.

"Or it was taken by something else," Maya whispered, glancing nervously around the room.

As we continued our search, the atmosphere grew more oppressive. The mansion seemed to be alive, its walls whispering secrets and shadows shifting in the corners of our vision. Each step felt heavier, as if we were wading through a fog of unease.

Suddenly, we heard a loud bang from upstairs. We froze, our breaths catching in our throats. "What was that?" Ethan asked, his voice barely a whisper.

"Let's check it out," Jade said, though her hands trembled.

We climbed the stairs, each creak of the floorboards echoing through the silence. At the top, we found ourselves in a long corridor lined with doors. The noise had come from the end of the hall.

We approached cautiously, our flashlights flickering. As we reached the door, it swung open on its own with a groan. Inside was a room filled with old furniture covered in white sheets. In the center was a large mirror, its surface cracked and dusty.

The mirror seemed to pulse with an eerie light, and as I stepped closer, I saw something moving in the reflection-a shadowy figure that wasn't there when I looked directly at it. My heart raced as the figure began to take shape, revealing a gaunt face with hollow eyes.

"Eliza?" I whispered, but the figure didn't respond. It just stared back at us, its expression sorrowful and intense.

"Is it trying to communicate?" Maya asked, her voice trembling.

"I don't know," I replied, feeling a cold sweat forming on my back. "But we need to be careful."

The figure in the mirror began to reach out, its hand stretching toward us. I felt a chill as the air grew colder. "We should leave," I said, trying to stay calm.

As we backed away, the mirror's surface shattered with a loud crash. We jumped, our flashlights casting erratic beams as we scrambled to escape. The mansion seemed to come alive around us, the walls creaking and groaning as if in protest of our intrusion.

We finally made it outside, gasping for breath. The mansion's dark silhouette loomed behind us, its windows like empty eyes watching our retreat.

"We need to figure out what's going on," Jade said, her voice shaking. "This place is dangerous."

"And we need to find that locket," I added. "It's the key to understanding what's happening."

As we walked away, the mansion faded into the darkness behind us, but its presence remained a looming threat. We had uncovered more than we had bargained for, and whatever was lurking in the mansion was far from done with us.

Chapter 6

The days following our harrowing visit to the mansion were filled with a mixture of dread and determination. We met every day after school, working together to piece together the fragments of the puzzle we had uncovered. Each night, my dreams grew darker, more vivid, and the presence of the mansion seemed to seep into every corner of my life.

Mr. Whitaker had been a huge help, providing us with access to additional records and offering guidance on what we might be dealing with. He was intrigued but remained cautious, knowing the potential dangers of diving into the supernatural.

One afternoon, as we sifted through more documents in the library, Jade made a breakthrough. "I found something that might explain what we're dealing with," she announced, her eyes wide with excitement and concern.

We gathered around her, peering at the documents she had spread out. "What is it?" Maya asked, her curiosity piqued.

"It's a detailed account of an exorcism performed at the mansion in the 1800s," Jade explained, pointing to a yellowed manuscript.

"Apparently, the Masons were involved in some sort of dark ritual, and the rival family-the Rooks-tried to intervene."

Ethan frowned. "So the curse was a result of a failed exorcism?"

"Not exactly," Jade replied. "It seems the Rooks' attempt to cleanse the mansion only made things worse. They inadvertently bound the malevolent entity to the house, making it more powerful."

"This sounds like it could explain the supernatural occurrences," I said, trying to piece it all together. "If the entity was bound to the mansion, it would be trapped there, feeding off the souls of anyone who entered."

"And if Eliza is one of those souls, she might be trapped because of this failed exorcism," Maya suggested, her face pale.

Jade nodded. "There's more. The manuscript mentions a specific ritual to break the curse, but it's incomplete. We're missing parts of it."

"We need to find the rest of it," Ethan said decisively. "If we can complete the ritual, we might be able to free Eliza and put an end to the haunting."

We spent the next few days researching every lead we could find. We visited local archives, talked to historians, and even contacted a few paranormal experts who might have insights into the rituals mentioned in the manuscript. Each attempt brought us closer but also deepened the mystery.

On Friday, we reconvened in the library, exhausted but hopeful. "We're running out of time," I said, glancing at the clock. "We need to get back to the mansion and find the rest of the ritual."

"I agree," Jade said. "But we need to be more prepared this time. We should take protective items and make sure we have a plan."

We spent the rest of the day gathering our supplies. We packed candles, salt, protective symbols, and cameras to document any evidence. As night approached, we met at the edge of the mansion's property, our equipment in tow.

The mansion looked even more menacing under the cover of darkness, its silhouette a dark monolith against the moonlit sky. We approached cautiously, our nerves on edge. The air was cold, and a heavy mist hung low over the ground.

We entered the mansion, our flashlights casting long shadows as we made our way to the main hall. The place felt different tonight-more oppressive, more alive. We set up our equipment and began our search.

Our strategy was to explore the rooms we hadn't investigated thoroughly before. We started with the basement, hoping to find any hidden compartments or clues. As we descended into the darkness, the air grew colder, and an unsettling silence enveloped us.

"Keep your eyes open," I said, my voice barely audible over the sound of our footsteps. "We're looking for anything unusual."

We searched the basement for hours, uncovering nothing more than old furniture and dusty crates. Just as we were about to give up, Ethan noticed something strange-a faint outline of a door hidden behind a stack of boxes.

We cleared the debris and opened the door, revealing a small, dimly lit room. Inside was an old chest covered in dust. The chest was bound with rusty chains, and a strange symbol was etched into its surface.

"This must be it," Jade said, her voice filled with awe. "It matches the symbol from the manuscript."

We carefully pried open the chest, revealing a collection of old, brittle documents and a small, ornate box. The documents looked ancient, and the box was adorned with intricate carvings.

"This box might contain the missing parts of the ritual," I said, feeling a mix of excitement and fear. "But we need to be cautious."

We opened the box, and inside were several scrolls and a small vial of dark liquid. The scrolls were covered in strange symbols and incantations, their pages yellowed with age. We carefully examined them, recognizing some of the symbols from the manuscript.

"Looks like we have the missing pieces," Jade said, her eyes shining with determination. "We need to perform the ritual exactly as described."

"We should do it in the main hall," Maya suggested. "It's the most central part of the mansion and might be the most effective place for the ritual."

We made our way back to the main hall, setting up the ritual components as described in the documents. The process was intricate, involving the arrangement of candles, salt, and the recitation of specific incantations.

As we worked, the atmosphere grew heavier. The mansion seemed to pulse with an eerie energy, and the shadows on the walls shifted in unsettling ways. Every creak and groan of the house felt like an omen.

We completed the ritual, reciting the final incantation with trembling voices. The air around us seemed to crackle with energy, and a cold wind swept through the hall. The candles flickered, and a deep, resonant voice echoed through the room, as if the mansion itself was reacting to our actions.

Suddenly, the temperature dropped sharply. We could see our breath in the air, and the shadows in the room seemed to come alive. The figure from my dreams appeared in the corner of the room, its eyes glowing with an intense, malevolent light.

"Eliza!" I shouted, hoping that our efforts had reached her.

The figure moved closer, its expression a mix of sorrow and anger. "You should not have come," it intoned, its voice a chilling whisper.

"We're trying to help," Jade said bravely, her voice steady despite the fear in her eyes. "We're trying to break the curse."

The figure's gaze seemed to soften, but the oppressive presence in the room remained. "The curse is ancient and powerful," Eliza's spirit said. "You cannot undo what has been done."

"We have to try," Ethan said, stepping forward. "We can't just leave you here."

The room seemed to grow darker, and the figure began to fade. "Beware," Eliza's voice echoed. "There are forces beyond your understanding. Not all is as it seems."

With those final words, the figure vanished, leaving us alone in the darkness. The oppressive presence lifted slightly, but the mansion remained eerily silent.

"We need to finish this," I said, feeling a renewed sense of urgency. "There's something else we're missing."

We gathered our equipment and left the mansion, our minds racing with questions and fears. The ritual had not provided the immediate results we hoped for, and the mansion's malevolent presence still loomed large.

As we drove home, I couldn't shake the feeling that we were on the brink of something much more dangerous than we had anticipated.

Eliza's warning echoed in my mind, and I knew we had to be more careful than ever.

The mansion's curse was far from over, and whatever was lurking in the shadows was far from finished with us.

Chapter 7

Maya

The excitement in the air was palpable as I walked into the library. Today, we were meeting with someone who might have the answers we desperately needed. After our last encounter at the mansion, it was clear that we were in over our heads. The mansion's dark presence wasn't something we could handle alone.

Jade and Ethan were already there, waiting with a mix of impatience and anxiety. Jade had been in touch with an old family friend, Professor Helen Roberts, a well-known paranormal researcher. Professor Roberts had agreed to meet us and offer her expertise.

"Hey, Maya," Ethan greeted me as I approached. "Ready for this?"

"As ready as I'll ever be," I replied. "I just hope she can help us."

Jade was already flipping through a notebook, her expression intense. "Professor Roberts should be here any minute now. I hope she's as knowledgeable as she sounds."

As if on cue, Professor Roberts entered the library, her presence commanding immediate respect. She was a tall woman with a no-nonsense demeanor and an air of authority. Her eyes were sharp and observant as she took in the room.

"Hello, everyone," she said, her voice steady. "I'm Professor Roberts. I hear you've been dealing with some unusual phenomena."

We introduced ourselves and explained our situation-the curse, the spirit of Eliza, and our recent experiences at the mansion. Professor Roberts listened intently, her brow furrowing as she took notes.

"This is quite a predicament," she said finally. "It sounds like you're dealing with a powerful and malevolent entity. The fact that the curse is tied to the mansion makes it even more complex."

"We were hoping you could help us understand the ritual we found," Jade said, pulling out the scrolls and documents. "We need to know how to complete it."

Professor Roberts examined the documents carefully, her eyes narrowing as she traced the symbols. "These are indeed part of a ritual, but they're incomplete. The missing elements are crucial for breaking the curse."

"Can you help us find the missing pieces?" I asked, feeling a sense of urgency.

"I can," Professor Roberts said. "But it won't be easy. We'll need to dig deeper into historical records and possibly consult other experts. The ritual's complexity suggests there might be more to the curse than you realize."

We spent the next hour discussing potential leads and strategies. Professor Roberts agreed to help us with research and provided us with additional tools for our investigation, including protective charms and a detailed guide on dealing with supernatural entities.

As we left the library, I felt a mix of relief and apprehension. We had a new ally, but the challenges ahead were still daunting. I knew we had to stay focused and work together to unravel the mansion's secrets.

Ethan

Later that day, I walked through the crowded school hallways, my mind racing. Meeting Professor Roberts had given us a new direction, but I couldn't shake the feeling that we were missing something crucial.

"Hey, Ethan!" I heard a familiar voice. It was Jake, a classmate I had known since middle school. "You look like you've got a lot on your mind."

"Just a bit," I replied, forcing a smile. "We've been dealing with some stuff lately."

Jake raised an eyebrow. "Stuff? You're not in trouble, are you?"

"Not exactly," I said, glancing around. "Just... dealing with some unusual situations."

Jake's curiosity was evident. "If you ever need to talk, I'm here. I might not have all the answers, but I can listen."

"Thanks, Jake," I said, appreciating the offer. "I might take you up on that."

As I continued down the hall, I couldn't help but wonder if Jake's offer might be more useful than I initially thought. We were tangled in something far beyond our understanding, and any support we could get would be valuable.

Back at home, I poured over the documents Professor Roberts had given us. There were detailed notes on protective rituals and countermeasures against malevolent entities. It was overwhelming, but we had no choice but to persevere.

I decided to focus on the protective charms. The more prepared we were, the better our chances of surviving the mansion's dangers. I carefully followed the instructions, hoping that the charms would provide some level of protection against the dark forces we were up against.

Jade

The next day at school, I found myself reflecting on the meeting with Professor Roberts. Her knowledge was invaluable, but I felt a growing sense of responsibility. We were on the brink of something big, and I needed to ensure we were prepared for whatever came next.

During lunch, I joined Maya and Ethan at our usual table. Maya was deep in thought, her eyes distant as she stared at her lunch. Ethan seemed preoccupied with his phone, likely reviewing the notes from our meeting with Professor Roberts.

"Hey, how's everyone holding up?" I asked, trying to gauge their moods.

"Trying to stay focused," Maya replied. "But I can't help but feel like we're missing something."

"I know what you mean," I said. "Professor Roberts mentioned that the curse might be more complex than we realize. We need to be thorough in our research."

Ethan nodded in agreement. "I've been going over the protective charms and rituals. It's a lot to take in, but we need to be ready for anything."

As we talked, I noticed a few students glancing over at us with curiosity. It was clear that something about our recent behavior was drawing attention. I tried to push aside my anxiety and focus on the task at hand. We couldn't afford to let anyone distract us or slow us down.

After lunch, we met in the library again, determined to make progress. The documents we had from Professor Roberts were extensive, and we needed to find the missing elements of the ritual quickly. We spent hours poring over old records and historical texts, hoping to uncover something that would help us complete the ritual.

The sense of urgency was growing. Each clue we found led to more questions, and the mansion's dark influence seemed to be closing in on us. We had to stay vigilant and keep pushing forward, no matter how daunting the task seemed.

Chapter 8

Jade

The sun was barely peeking over the horizon as I approached the mansion, the first light casting long, eerie shadows across the overgrown lawn. The once-grand estate now looked like a relic from another era, with ivy-clad walls and broken windows that seemed to watch us with a silent, accusing stare.

The sense of foreboding was almost palpable, as if the house itself was breathing heavily, awaiting our arrival. I glanced at Maya and Ethan, who flanked me, their expressions reflecting the same mix of determination and trepidation I felt.

"This place gets creepier every time we come here," Maya murmured, adjusting her backpack filled with supplies. "Are we sure this is a good idea?"

"We don't have much choice," I replied, trying to sound more confident than I felt. "We need to find the missing parts of the ritual, and this is our best lead."

The mansion's front door creaked open with a groan, as though reluctant to let us in. We stepped inside, the musty smell of decay enveloping us. Dust motes danced in the beams of our flashlights, and the air felt thick with a stifling silence.

We made our way to the study, the room where we had found the old chest previously. The heavy wooden door seemed to resist our attempts to open it, but with a final push, it gave way. The room beyond was cluttered with old books and forgotten artifacts, each one a testament to the mansion's long and troubled history.

"This place is like a maze," Ethan said, his voice echoing off the walls as he shone his flashlight over a row of dusty shelves. "How are we supposed to find anything in here?"

"We'll have to be systematic," I said, starting to sift through the piles of books and papers. "Let's check every corner and see if there's anything we missed last time."

Hours passed as we combed through the study, our hands growing dusty and our patience wearing thin. Just as we were about to take a break, Maya let out a soft exclamation. "Look at this!"

She had uncovered a hidden compartment behind a bookcase. The compartment was filled with old, leather-bound journals and a small, ornate box similar to the one we had found before. My heart raced as we carefully opened the box.

Inside were several old scrolls, each one meticulously detailed. The symbols and incantations matched those from the incomplete ritual we had found earlier. Our hearts lifted with renewed hope.

"This could be it," Ethan said, his eyes gleaming with excitement. "We might have found the missing pieces."

Maya

With the scrolls in hand, we decided to take a closer look at the mansion's history. We returned to the library, where the quiet ambiance felt oddly comforting after the mansion's oppressive atmosphere.

As we spread the scrolls out on a large table, Professor Roberts joined us. She examined the documents with keen interest, her eyes tracing the symbols with practiced ease.

"These scrolls are significant," she said, her voice steady. "They appear to complete the ritual. We need to decipher the remaining incantations and determine the exact procedure."

We worked together, deciphering the ancient text and cross-referencing it with historical records. The ritual involved creating a protective barrier and invoking a series of complex incantations to break the curse. It was intricate and demanding, requiring precise timing and coordination.

As we worked, Professor Roberts shared more about the mansion's history. "The Masons were known for their involvement in occult practices," she explained. "Their rituals often had unintended consequences, and this curse may be the result of one such failed attempt."

The more we learned, the more the gravity of our task became apparent. The mansion's history was marred by dark rituals and unresolved conflicts. The curse was not just a supernatural occurrence but a culmination of human ambition and failure.

Ethan

As night fell, we prepared for another visit to the mansion. The air outside was crisp, and the moonlight cast long, silvery shadows across the landscape. The mansion loomed in the distance, its dark silhouette a stark contrast against the star-filled sky.

We approached the mansion with our supplies-candles, salt, protective symbols, and the newly discovered scrolls. The atmosphere was tense, the weight of our task settling heavily on our shoulders.

Inside, the mansion seemed even more foreboding. The shadows seemed to shift and writhe as if alive, and the silence was occasionally broken by the distant creaks and groans of the old house. We made our way to the main hall, where we set up our ritual components with meticulous care.

"Let's be careful," I said, feeling a twinge of unease. "We need to get this right."

We began the ritual, arranging the candles in a precise pattern and reciting the incantations from the scrolls. The air grew colder, and an eerie wind whipped through the hall, extinguishing some of the candles.

"Stay focused!" I shouted, trying to keep everyone on track. "We need to finish this before the energy gets too chaotic."

As we continued, the temperature dropped sharply, and a low, rumbling sound filled the hall. The shadows around us seemed to darken, and the walls appeared to pulse with an otherworldly energy. A figure materialized in the corner of the room, its presence a chilling reminder of the curse's power.

Jade

The figure was unmistakably Eliza, her ghostly form flickering in and out of view. Her eyes were filled with a mixture of sorrow and desperation as she watched us.

"We're close," she seemed to say, though her voice was more of a haunting whisper than actual words. "Finish the ritual."

We pressed on, our voices trembling as we recited the final incantations. The energy in the room reached a crescendo, the air crackling with raw power. A brilliant light erupted from the candles, and the mansion seemed to tremble in response.

Suddenly, the oppressive atmosphere began to lift. The shadows receded, and the temperature slowly returned to normal. The figure of Eliza faded, leaving behind a sense of peace and calm.

"We did it," Maya said, her voice a mix of relief and exhaustion. "I think we've finally broken the curse."

As we gathered our things and prepared to leave, I couldn't shake the feeling that our work was far from over. The mansion was still a place of dark memories and unresolved conflicts. Our victory was a significant step, but there were still many unanswered questions.

We left the mansion, the night air feeling lighter and less oppressive. The experience had changed us, and I knew we would carry the weight of our encounter with the mansion for a long time.

Chapter 9

Maya

The morning sun filtered through the curtains of my room, casting warm, golden light across the cluttered desk where the scrolls and notes were spread out. Despite the peaceful scene outside, I couldn't shake the feeling of unease that had settled over me since our last visit to the mansion.

The ritual had been intense, and while we had made progress, there were still many unanswered questions. Eliza's appearance was a stark reminder of the unresolved nature of the curse. I needed to find more information to fully understand what we were dealing with.

I decided to visit the local historical society. They had extensive archives that might hold clues about the Mason family and the mansion's dark history. Armed with a notebook and a list of questions, I headed out.

The historical society was housed in a quaint, brick building, its front lawn lined with old-fashioned lampposts and flowerbeds.

Inside, the air was filled with the musty scent of old paper and leather. Mrs. Thompson, the curator, greeted me with a warm smile.

"Good morning, Maya," she said. "How can I assist you today?"

"I'm researching the Mason family and their mansion," I explained. "I need to find out more about their history and any unusual events that might have happened here."

Mrs. Thompson led me to a section of the archives filled with old newspapers, family records, and personal letters. I set to work, flipping through yellowed pages and faded documents. Most of the records were mundane, detailing everyday life and business dealings, but I was determined to find something relevant.

After several hours, I came across a series of newspaper articles about a tragic fire that had occurred at the mansion decades ago. The articles mentioned that the fire had been suspicious, with rumors of arson and supernatural involvement. This seemed like a significant lead.

I photocopied the relevant articles and thanked Mrs. Thompson for her help. As I left the historical society, I felt a surge of excitement. The fire might have been a pivotal event related to the curse, and understanding it could bring us closer to solving the mystery.

Ethan

Later that day, I met Maya and Jade at the library to share what I'd found. We gathered in our usual study nook, surrounded by stacks of books and our various research materials.

"Hey, I've got something," Maya said, setting down a folder with the photocopied articles. "I found some old newspaper articles about a fire at the mansion. It seems like there was something unusual about it."

Jade and I leaned in, scanning the articles. The reports were unsettling-accounts of strange occurrences leading up to the fire and mentions of the Mason family's involvement in occult practices. It was clear that something significant had happened.

"This fire could be linked to the curse," I said, my mind racing with possibilities. "Maybe it was part of a failed ritual or a cover-up for something even darker."

"We need to find more details about the fire," Jade suggested. "If it was related to the curse, understanding what happened could help us figure out the missing pieces of the ritual."

As we discussed our next steps, I noticed Jade's phone buzzing. She glanced at it, her expression turning serious. "It's Professor Roberts. She wants to meet us at the library."

We made our way to the library's special collections room, where Professor Roberts was already waiting. She looked concerned as we entered.

"I've been reviewing the documents you brought," she said, showing us a set of old, handwritten letters. "These letters were written by a member of the Mason family. They provide insight into their activities and the events leading up to the fire."

The letters described the Mason family's growing obsession with dark rituals and their attempts to harness supernatural powers. The final letter mentioned a secret ritual intended to grant immortality, but something had gone terribly wrong.

"This is crucial information," Professor Roberts said. "It confirms that the curse was a result of a failed ritual. The fire might have been an attempt to cover up the consequences."

We spent the rest of the day analyzing the letters and cross-referencing them with the newspaper articles. The more we uncovered, the clearer it became that the mansion's history was even darker than we had imagined.

The realization that the Mason family's actions had led to the curse and the fire made the stakes even higher. We were no longer just dealing with a supernatural entity; we were confronting the legacy of a powerful and dangerous family.

Jade

As evening approached, we decided to return to the mansion with our newfound information. The sun was setting, casting an orange glow over the landscape. The mansion's silhouette was stark against the fading light, a reminder of the darkness we were up against.

We approached the mansion, the air growing colder as we neared. The atmosphere was thick with anticipation and apprehension. Our plan was to use the information from the letters to locate any remaining traces of the ritual and the Mason family's activities.

Inside, the mansion felt even more oppressive than before. The shadows seemed to press in on us, and the silence was occasionally broken by the distant creaks of the old structure.

We made our way to the basement, where we had previously found the hidden compartment. The basement was cold and damp, with a faint, musty smell that seemed to cling to everything. We set up our equipment and began searching for any additional clues.

As we sifted through old boxes and dusty shelves, a sudden noise made us jump. It was a low, raspy whisper, almost like a breath against the ear. We exchanged nervous glances, our flashlights sweeping the dark corners of the basement.

"Did anyone else hear that?" Maya asked, her voice barely above a whisper.

"I heard it," Ethan replied, his face pale. "It sounded like it came from over there."

We moved cautiously toward the source of the noise, our hearts pounding in our chests. The basement seemed to grow colder with each step, and the oppressive feeling of being watched returned.

Suddenly, a shadowy figure appeared at the edge of the room. It was a fleeting glimpse, but it was enough to send chills down our spines. The figure seemed to vanish as quickly as it had appeared, leaving us in stunned silence.

"Let's stay focused," I said, trying to keep my voice steady. "We need to find whatever is left of the ritual."

We continued our search, determined to uncover the final pieces of the puzzle. The mansion's dark history and the supernatural forces at play were closing in on us, but we couldn't afford to back down now. The truth was within our grasp, and we were determined to see it through to the end.

Chapter 10

<hr>

Maya

The night was still as we approached the mansion for what felt like the hundredth time. The moonlight bathed the house in a cold, silvery glow, casting long shadows that seemed to move with a life of their own. We were armed with new information and a sense of urgency that pressed heavily on us.

Inside, the mansion felt colder than before, the air thick with anticipation. We made our way to the library, where we planned to analyze the latest clues. The tension between us was palpable, and I couldn't ignore the subtle glances that Ethan and Jade exchanged. There was something unspoken between them, a current that added an extra layer of unease.

"Let's get to work," I said, trying to focus on the task at hand. "We need to decipher these notes and find the missing elements of the ritual."

As we set up our workspace, Jade seemed unusually quiet, her focus on the documents with a furrowed brow. Ethan, on the other hand, appeared distracted, his eyes occasionally drifting toward Jade.

"Is everything okay?" I asked Jade, concerned by her silence.

"Yeah, just... a lot on my mind," she replied, her voice low. "We need to be thorough with this."

Ethan nodded in agreement but didn't say much. There was an awkwardness in the air, a sense that something unsaid was hanging between us.

We spent the next few hours sifting through the documents and cross-referencing them with our previous findings. The mansion's oppressive atmosphere seemed to press down on us, making the work feel heavier than usual.

Ethan

It was hard to concentrate on the ritual's details with the growing tension between Jade and me. I couldn't deny the feelings that had been developing over the past few weeks-feelings that seemed to become more complicated with every passing day.

Jade and I had always been close, but now there was something more, something unspoken. I could see it in the way she glanced at me when she thought I wasn't looking, and in the moments of quiet we shared.

As we worked side by side, I noticed the way her fingers brushed against mine when she reached for a document. It was a small touch, almost accidental, but it sent a jolt through me. I tried to focus on the task, but my thoughts kept drifting back to her.

"You okay?" Jade's voice broke through my thoughts, her concern evident. "You seem a bit distracted."

"Just a lot on my mind," I replied, forcing a smile. "We're so close to figuring this out. I just want to get it right."

Jade's gaze lingered on me for a moment before she returned to her work. There was a softness in her eyes that made my heart race, despite the tension we were under.

We worked late into the night, our progress slow but steady. The ritual's details were coming together, but there was still a lot left to uncover. The mansion's dark presence seemed to loom over us, a constant reminder of the stakes.

Jade

As we wrapped up for the night, I found myself alone with Ethan in the library. The others had left to take a break, and the silence between us was both comforting and unnerving.

"Jade," Ethan said, his voice low. "I need to talk to you about something."

I looked up from the documents, my heart skipping a beat. "Sure, what's up?"

Ethan hesitated for a moment, his eyes searching mine. "I... I know things have been intense lately, and I can't ignore what I'm feeling anymore."

Before I could respond, the air around us seemed to grow colder. The shadows in the library seemed to shift and darken, casting eerie shapes on the walls.

"Do you hear that?" I asked, my voice trembling slightly.

Ethan nodded, his expression serious. "Yeah, I do. It sounds like... whispering."

We both turned toward the source of the sound. The whispers grew louder, more distinct, and a chill ran down my spine. It was as if the mansion itself was reacting to our conversation.

"I guess we'll have to put this on hold," Ethan said, his voice steady despite the eerie atmosphere. "We need to focus on the ritual."

I nodded, trying to push my feelings aside. We returned to our work, but the moment between us lingered, adding an extra layer of complexity to our already difficult situation.

As the night wore on, we made significant progress on the ritual. The details were falling into place, and we felt a sense of accomplishment despite the looming darkness.

Maya

The following day, we gathered at the library again, determined to finish what we had started. The atmosphere was still heavy, but the progress we had made gave us hope.

"I think we're getting close," I said, spreading out the final notes. "We just need to finalize the ritual and prepare for the final confrontation."

Jade and Ethan exchanged another glance, their faces reflecting a mix of exhaustion and determination. I couldn't ignore the subtle tension between them, but I pushed it to the back of my mind. We had more pressing concerns to address.

We spent the day preparing for the ritual, gathering the necessary materials and finalizing the incantations. The process was meticulous, but we were determined to get it right.

As evening approached, we felt a renewed sense of urgency. The mansion's darkness seemed to close in around us, and the air was thick with anticipation.

We made our way back to the mansion, ready to face whatever awaited us. The hints of romance between Jade and Ethan were just a whisper compared to the louder, more pressing dangers we faced. But I knew that the feelings they harbored would eventually come to the forefront, adding another layer to the complex web of our lives.

Chapter 11

Jade

The mansion loomed ahead, its dark silhouette a stark contrast against the evening sky. The weight of the past few weeks seemed to hang heavily in the air, and the tension was palpable. As we approached the mansion, my thoughts kept drifting back to the unfinished conversation with Ethan. There was a growing complexity to our feelings that we hadn't yet fully addressed.

We entered the mansion, the familiar chill settling over us. The house seemed quieter than usual, the silence almost oppressive. We made our way to the basement, where we had previously discovered the hidden compartment. Our goal was to finalize the ritual and put an end to the curse once and for all.

"Okay, let's get everything set up," I said, trying to sound more confident than I felt. "We need to be precise."

Ethan and Maya set about arranging the ritual components, their movements methodical and focused. The atmosphere was heavy with anticipation, and I could sense the strain in their movements.

"Jade," Ethan said, his voice low as he adjusted a candle. "I know we've been through a lot, and I just wanted to say-"

A sudden noise interrupted him-a faint scratching sound coming from behind a wall. We all froze, our eyes wide. The sound seemed to be coming from the same direction as the whispers we had heard before.

"Did anyone else hear that?" Maya asked, her voice barely above a whisper.

"I heard it," I said, feeling a shiver run down my spine. "It's coming from over there."

We approached the source of the sound, our flashlights illuminating the old, dusty walls. The scratching grew louder, and with a collective effort, we pushed against the wall. It creaked and groaned, revealing a hidden passage.

"This must be it," Ethan said, his eyes gleaming with a mixture of excitement and apprehension. "The missing chamber."

We entered the passage, which was narrow and dimly lit. The walls were lined with strange symbols, and the air was musty and cold. As we moved further in, the passage opened into a large chamber, its walls adorned with intricate carvings and ancient symbols.

"This is incredible," Maya said, her eyes wide as she took in the chamber's details. "It's like stepping back in time."

The chamber was filled with old, dusty artifacts and remnants of past rituals. In the center of the room was an ornate pedestal with an ancient tome resting on it.

"We need to examine that book," I said, moving closer. "It might hold the final pieces of the ritual."

Ethan

As Jade and Maya approached the pedestal, I couldn't shake the feeling that something was off. The air in the chamber felt heavy, almost charged with a latent energy. I stayed close to Jade, my senses on high alert.

The tome on the pedestal was bound in dark leather, its cover adorned with symbols that matched those we had encountered throughout our research. Jade carefully opened the book, revealing pages filled with detailed instructions and arcane text.

"This could be it," Jade said, her voice filled with a mix of relief and excitement. "The final steps of the ritual."

As we examined the tome, the chamber seemed to grow colder. The shadows on the walls shifted and writhed, creating eerie patterns that seemed almost alive. A low, resonant hum filled the air, adding to the chamber's unsettling atmosphere.

"We need to be careful," I said, trying to keep my voice steady. "If this is the final step, we need to follow the instructions precisely."

We began to decipher the book's contents, noting the detailed procedures and incantations. The ritual involved a series of complex steps, including the placement of specific artifacts and the recitation of powerful incantations.

As we worked, I couldn't help but steal glances at Jade. Her concentration was intense, and I could see the strain and determination in her eyes. Despite the gravity of our situation, I found myself drawn to her, and the unspoken connection between us seemed to grow stronger.

Jade

As we prepared for the ritual, I felt a surge of anticipation and anxiety. The final steps were crucial, and the pressure was mounting. I glanced at Ethan, who was working beside me. There was an unspoken understanding between us, a sense of solidarity that I found comforting.

"Jade," Ethan said quietly, his voice almost lost in the hum of the chamber. "No matter what happens, I want you to know that I'm here for you."

His words caught me off guard, and I looked up, meeting his gaze. There was a sincerity in his eyes that made my heart skip a beat. For a moment, the weight of the curse and the darkness of the mansion seemed to fade, leaving only the intensity of the moment between us.

"Thanks, Ethan," I said softly, trying to keep my voice steady. "I appreciate it."

As we completed the final preparations, the chamber seemed to come alive with a palpable energy. The symbols on the walls glowed faintly, and the air crackled with an otherworldly presence.

"We're ready," Maya said, her voice determined. "Let's start the ritual."

We began the incantations, our voices echoing through the chamber. The atmosphere grew increasingly charged, and the energy in the room seemed to build to a crescendo. The final steps of the ritual were delicate and demanding, requiring precise timing and coordination.

As we reached the final incantation, the chamber's energy reached its peak. A brilliant light erupted from the center of the room, enveloping us in a warm, comforting glow. The oppressive darkness that had lingered seemed to dissipate, replaced by a sense of peace and calm.

We completed the ritual, and the chamber fell silent. The shadows on the walls receded, and the eerie hum faded, leaving behind a sense of tranquility.

"That's it," Maya said, her voice filled with relief. "I think we've done it."

We looked around the chamber, our faces reflecting a mix of exhaustion and satisfaction. The mansion's curse had been lifted, and the sense of accomplishment was palpable.

As we made our way back to the main hall, I couldn't help but reflect on the journey we had been through. The mansion's dark history was behind us, and the unspoken feelings between Ethan and me remained a subtle but significant part of our experience.

Chapter 12

J ade

The following morning, the mansion seemed different. The oppressive atmosphere that had clung to every corner was now replaced by a subtle sense of calm. It felt as though the mansion itself was breathing a sigh of relief, its dark secrets finally laid to rest.

We gathered in the library to review our findings and discuss our next steps. The sunlight streaming through the tall windows cast a warm glow over the room, a stark contrast to the cold, eerie light we had worked under the previous night.

"I think we've done everything we can," Maya said, her voice tinged with exhaustion but also relief. "The ritual should have lifted the curse."

Ethan nodded in agreement, though his expression was thoughtful. "We still need to make sure the effects are permanent. It's possible there could be residual effects or hidden consequences."

I looked at Ethan, feeling a mix of emotions. The intensity of our shared experience had brought us closer, and there was an unspoken bond between us that I wasn't sure how to address. As much as I wanted to talk about it, there was a part of me that hesitated.

"Let's do a final sweep of the mansion," I suggested, trying to keep my tone practical. "We should make sure there are no lingering issues before we leave."

We spent the day thoroughly inspecting the mansion. The sense of unease had dissipated, and the mansion's grand, faded beauty was starting to re-emerge. It was almost as if the house was shedding its old skin, revealing something new beneath.

Ethan

As we moved through the mansion, I couldn't help but feel a sense of finality. The ritual had been a monumental task, and seeing it through had left me both relieved and introspective. My thoughts often drifted back to Jade. Her presence had been a constant source of strength throughout our ordeal, and the subtle moments we shared had left a lasting impression on me.

We reached the library, where Maya was busy organizing the documents we had collected. Jade and I found a quiet corner, away from the others, to discuss our findings and what lay ahead.

"Jade," I began, trying to find the right words. "About last night..."

Jade looked up, her eyes meeting mine with a mix of curiosity and apprehension. "Yes?"

"I just wanted to say," I continued, searching for the right words, "that I'm glad we went through this together. You've been incredible, and I..."

Before I could finish, Maya's voice cut in from across the room. "Hey, you two, come over here. I think I found something important."

Jade and I exchanged a look, the moment between us interrupted but not forgotten. We moved to join Maya, who had uncovered a hidden compartment in one of the library's old bookshelves. Inside was a small, ornate box, its surface covered in intricate designs.

"This must be something we missed," Maya said, her eyes wide with excitement. "Let's see what's inside."

We opened the box, revealing a collection of old letters and personal items. The letters were from members of the Mason family, detailing their experiences and the events leading up to the curse.

"These letters provide a personal perspective on the curse," Maya explained. "They might offer more insight into the family's motivations and actions."

We spent the next few hours reading through the letters, piecing together the story of the Mason family's downfall. The letters revealed the depth of their obsession with the occult and their desperation to escape the consequences of their actions. It was a sobering reminder of the human element behind the curse.

Jade

As we read through the letters, I felt a growing sense of empathy for the Mason family, despite their dark deeds. Their story was one of ambition and hubris, and their ultimate downfall was a tragic reminder of the dangers of tampering with forces beyond our control.

Ethan sat beside me, his focus on the letters. I could sense the tension between us, the words left unspoken hanging in the air. The shared experience had brought us closer, and the moments we had shared felt more significant than ever.

After finishing the letters, we decided to take a break. The mansion's grandeur was more apparent in the daylight, and I found myself wandering through the hallways, reflecting on our journey.

Ethan joined me, his presence both comforting and distracting. We walked in silence for a while, the quiet broken only by the soft creaks of the old house.

"I've been thinking about what you said last night," I said finally, breaking the silence. "And... I'm grateful for everything we've been through together."

Ethan looked at me, his expression softening. "Me too, Jade. This experience has been... intense, but it's also brought us closer."

We stopped by a large window, looking out over the mansion's grounds. The view was serene, a stark contrast to the turmoil we had faced.

"I guess we'll have to figure out what comes next," Ethan said, his voice thoughtful. "There's still a lot to process."

"Yeah," I agreed. "But for now, I'm just glad we made it through."

As we stood there, the tension between us seemed to ease. The shared experience had created a bond that was both deep and complex. We didn't have all the answers, but we had each other, and that was a start.

Maya

As evening approached, we gathered in the library for one final meeting. The mansion was quiet, its dark past finally laid to rest. The atmosphere was one of cautious optimism, and the weight of our task was beginning to lift.

"We've done everything we can," Maya said, her voice filled with a sense of accomplishment. "The curse is lifted, and the mansion is free of its dark influence."

We all nodded in agreement, the sense of relief palpable. The letters and artifacts we had uncovered provided closure to the mystery, and the mansion's oppressive atmosphere had been replaced by a sense of peace.

"Thank you," I said, looking at Maya and Ethan. "For everything. This has been a challenging experience, but we made it through together."

Ethan and Maya both smiled, their expressions reflecting a mix of relief and satisfaction. We had faced the darkness and emerged stronger, and the bonds we had formed would endure beyond the mansion's walls.

As we prepared to leave, I glanced back at the mansion, its grand façade now bathed in the soft glow of the setting sun. The journey had been intense, but it had also been a reminder of the strength we found in each other.

Chapter 13

Jade

The mansion was finally behind us. As we drove away, the feeling of relief was almost palpable. The sun was setting, casting a warm, golden hue over the landscape. It felt like a fresh start, a new chapter in our lives after the darkness we had just left behind.

We had decided to head to a nearby town for a well-deserved break before heading back to our normal lives. The town was quaint and charming, a stark contrast to the eerie mansion we had spent so much time in.

"I can't believe it's finally over," Maya said, her voice filled with a mixture of exhaustion and satisfaction. "It feels like a weight has been lifted."

"It does," Ethan agreed. "But I think we need to take some time to process everything."

We checked into a cozy bed-and-breakfast, the warm, inviting atmosphere a welcome change from the cold, oppressive environment of the mansion. The owner, a kindly woman named Mrs.

Thompson, greeted us with a warm smile and showed us to our rooms.

"I'll grab us some dinner," I said, heading out to explore the town. "Let's meet back here in an hour."

As I walked through the town's charming streets, I felt a sense of freedom I hadn't experienced in weeks. The normalcy of the town was a stark contrast to the chaos we had faced, and I found myself appreciating the simple pleasures of everyday life.

Ethan

After Jade left, Maya and I decided to take a stroll around the town. It was a small place with a friendly, relaxed vibe, and the change of pace was refreshing.

"So," Maya said as we walked, "what do you think about everything that happened? It's been quite a journey."

"I'm still processing it," I admitted. "It's hard to believe it's over. We went through so much, and now it feels like we're finally catching our breath."

Maya nodded. "It was intense, but I think we learned a lot. About the curse, about ourselves... and about each other."

I glanced at Maya, noting the thoughtful expression on her face. "Yeah, we did. And I think the experience brought us closer."

The conversation shifted to lighter topics as we wandered through the town, but my thoughts kept drifting back to Jade. The moments we had shared in the mansion had left a lasting impression on me, and I found myself thinking about what might come next.

When we returned to the bed-and-breakfast, Jade had already arrived with dinner. The meal was simple but delicious, and we sat around the table, enjoying the comfort of a normal evening.

"Let's relax tonight," Jade suggested. "We've earned it."

Ethan

We spent the evening talking and laughing, the camaraderie of our shared experience bringing us closer. The atmosphere was relaxed, and the conversation flowed easily.

At one point, I caught Ethan's eye, and the connection between us felt stronger than ever. There was something unspoken but palpable, a mutual understanding that went beyond words.

After dinner, Maya suggested we explore the town's small park, which was beautifully lit and perfect for a leisurely stroll. We walked together, the cool evening air refreshing after our time in the mansion.

As we strolled through the park, Ethan and I found ourselves walking side by side. The closeness of our bodies and the soft murmur of the conversation created an intimate atmosphere.

"Jade," Ethan said softly, "I've been thinking a lot about what we went through. It's made me realize how important certain things are... and certain people."

I looked at him, my heart skipping a beat. "Like what?"

"Like how we've all been through so much together," Ethan said, his voice earnest. "And how that's changed the way I see things... and people."

I could feel the intensity of his words, and it made me realize how much our shared experience had impacted me as well. We were standing close, the park's soft lights casting a gentle glow around us.

"I feel the same way," I admitted. "It's been an intense journey, but it's also brought us closer."

There was a moment of silence between us, filled with unspoken feelings and shared understanding. The connection between us was undeniable, and it felt like we were on the cusp of something new.

Maya

As I watched Jade and Ethan, I could sense the shift in their dynamic. The bond they shared was evident, and it seemed to be growing stronger. The experience had clearly had a profound impact on both of them.

I decided to give them some space, opting to take a seat on a nearby bench and enjoy the peaceful surroundings. The park was tranquil, and the soft rustle of leaves in the breeze created a calming atmosphere.

I pulled out my phone and started browsing through some of the photos we had taken during our investigation. The images brought back memories of our time in the mansion, and I felt a mix of nostalgia and relief.

When Jade and Ethan returned to the bench, their faces were reflective but content. The evening had been a welcome break from the intensity of our recent experiences.

"It's nice to have a moment to just... be," Maya said, smiling at them.

"Yeah," Jade agreed. "It's been a long road, but it's good to have this time to relax."

We spent the rest of the evening enjoying each other's company, the sense of camaraderie and friendship strong among us. The bond we had formed through our shared experiences was something that would stay with us, no matter where life took us next.

As the night wore on, we headed back to the bed-and-breakfast, feeling a renewed sense of hope and possibility. The journey we had been on was over, but the connections we had made would continue to grow and evolve.

Chapter 14

E than
The next morning, we were greeted by the crisp, clear air of the small town. The recent events still lingered in my mind, and as we enjoyed a hearty breakfast at the bed-and-breakfast, the conversation naturally turned to our next steps.

"So," Maya began, sipping her coffee. "What's the plan now? Do we head back to school or take a bit more time off?"

I glanced at Jade, who seemed deep in thought. Her recent experiences had left her more contemplative than usual, and I could sense that she was trying to piece together her thoughts about our time at the mansion.

"I think we should head back to school," Jade finally said. "We've accomplished a lot, but there's still a lot to process and some things to take care of."

"Agreed," Maya said. "But maybe we could use a couple of days to unwind before diving back into the routine."

"I'm all for that," I said. "A few days to regroup wouldn't hurt. It's been a whirlwind of activity."

After breakfast, we decided to take a leisurely tour of the town, exploring the local shops and enjoying the relaxed atmosphere. It was a welcome break from the tension we had been under, and it gave us a chance to unwind and appreciate the simpler things in life.

As we wandered through a quaint antique shop, I noticed Jade lingering near a display of old photographs. The images were black-and-white, depicting scenes from a bygone era. I joined her, intrigued by the nostalgia in her eyes.

"Find something interesting?" I asked.

Jade nodded, holding up a photograph. "Look at this. It's a picture of the mansion from back in the day. It's incredible how much it's changed."

The photograph showed the mansion in its prime, its grandeur evident even in the faded image. The lush gardens and pristine facade were a stark contrast to the dilapidated state we had seen.

"It's like seeing the mansion in its glory days," I said, admiring the photo. "It must have been quite something."

Jade sighed, a mixture of awe and sadness in her expression. "It's a reminder of how much things have changed. The mansion's history is so rich, but it's also been marred by darkness."

We continued our exploration, and as the day wore on, the sense of normalcy was both comforting and bittersweet. The town's charm was a stark contrast to the mansion's oppressive atmosphere, but it also made me realize how much we had been through.

Jade

In the afternoon, we visited a local park with beautiful gardens. It was a peaceful place, perfect for reflection. We took a seat on a bench, enjoying the tranquility and the beauty of our surroundings.

"I've been thinking a lot about everything we went through," I said, breaking the comfortable silence. "It's hard to believe it's all behind us."

"It is," Maya agreed. "But I think we've all grown from the experience. We've faced something truly extraordinary."

Ethan nodded, his gaze thoughtful. "I agree. And I think we've also learned a lot about ourselves and each other. It's been a journey of discovery."

We spent the rest of the day relaxing in the park, enjoying the simple pleasures of the moment. It was a chance to reconnect and appreciate the bond we had formed.

As evening approached, we headed back to the bed-and-breakfast, ready to enjoy a quiet dinner and prepare for our return to school. The time we spent in the town had been a welcome respite, and it had given us the chance to reflect on our journey.

Maya

That evening, we gathered in the common room of the bed-and-breakfast, the warmth of the fire and the comfort of the surroundings creating a cozy atmosphere. We talked about our plans for the future and what we wanted to achieve next.

"I'm looking forward to getting back to a normal routine," Maya said, stretching out on one of the plush sofas. "But I'm also excited about the possibilities that lie ahead."

Jade and Ethan nodded in agreement, the sense of relief and accomplishment still fresh. The experience had changed us, and we were all looking forward to what came next, albeit with a newfound appreciation for the ordinary.

"I think we've earned a little break before jumping back into school," Jade said. "Maybe we should use this time to set some new goals and think about what we want to do next."

"Sounds like a good plan," Ethan agreed. "It's important to take a moment to reflect and plan for the future."

We spent the evening discussing our goals and dreams, the conversation flowing easily as we shared our hopes and aspirations. The camaraderie among us was strong, and the bond we had formed through our shared experiences was evident.

As the night wore on, we eventually retired to our rooms, feeling a sense of contentment and closure. The journey had been intense, but it had also brought us closer together, and we were ready to face whatever came next with renewed strength and clarity.

Jade

The next morning, we packed up and prepared to head back to school. The town had been a much-needed break, and we felt ready to return to our normal lives. As we drove away, the familiar landscape of home seemed both comforting and surreal.

"I think we're all ready for this next chapter," Maya said from the back seat, her voice filled with anticipation.

"Absolutely," Ethan agreed. "We've been through a lot, but we've come out stronger. I'm looking forward to seeing how we apply what we've learned."

As we approached the school, the familiar sight of the campus was a welcome relief. The routine of classes and the presence of friends felt reassuring after our recent experiences.

Ethan

Returning to school was both comforting and challenging. The familiar routine was a stark contrast to the intense experiences we had endured, and it took some time to readjust.

We reunited with our friends, who were eager to hear about our adventure. We shared only the basics, keeping the more intense details to ourselves. The experience had bonded us in ways that went beyond words, and we were content to leave some aspects of our journey private.

"Welcome back!" one of our friends, Laura, greeted us with a hug. "We missed you guys!"

"It's good to be back," Jade said, her smile genuine. "We've had quite the adventure, but we're glad to be home."

As we settled back into our school routine, we found comfort in the familiar surroundings and the supportive presence of our friends. The mansion and its mysteries were behind us, but the lessons we had learned and the connections we had made would stay with us.

Jade

One afternoon, as I walked across campus, I ran into Ethan. We exchanged a warm smile, the bond between us evident in the way we interacted.

"Hey," I said, falling into step beside him. "How's it going?"

"Good," Ethan replied, his tone relaxed. "It feels like we're finally settling back into normal life."

"I know what you mean," I agreed. "It's strange how quickly things can return to normal, but I'm glad we have a sense of closure."

We walked together, discussing our classes and catching up on schoolwork. The transition back to normalcy was smooth, and the support of our friends made it easier.

Maya

Life at school resumed its usual rhythm, but the experience at the mansion had left its mark on all of us. We were more connected than ever, and the shared journey had given us a new perspective on life and each other.

We continued to support each other, both academically and personally. The challenges we had faced had strengthened our friendship, and we were determined to make the most of the new opportunities that lay ahead.

As the weeks went by, we found ourselves reflecting on our adventure with a sense of accomplishment and gratitude. The experience had been transformative, and we were ready to embrace the future with a renewed sense of purpose.

Chapter 15

Jade

The first few weeks back at school felt like a whirlwind of normalcy. The thrill and danger of our recent adventure seemed like a distant memory as we settled into our routines. However, the sense of unease that had lingered ever since our return was difficult to shake. It felt like something was just on the edge of our perception, waiting to resurface.

One crisp autumn afternoon, as I walked across the campus, I noticed something strange near the old library. There was a flyer pinned to the bulletin board, its faded edges fluttering in the breeze. It caught my eye because it had a familiar feel to it-something about the design and the handwriting seemed eerily reminiscent of the cryptic messages we had encountered before.

I pulled the flyer from the board and examined it closely. It was an invitation to a mysterious "history night" event at a nearby historical society, detailing an investigation into the town's forgotten legends. The event was scheduled for the following weekend.

I took a deep breath. The flyer's resemblance to our previous encounters with the supernatural made my heart race. Could this be another clue or perhaps something more?

Ethan

Later that day, I met up with Jade and Maya in the cafeteria. They were discussing their plans for the weekend, and I decided to bring up the flyer.

"Hey, I found something odd today," I said, showing them the flyer. "It's for a history night at the local historical society. It seems kind of... familiar."

Jade looked at the flyer, her eyes narrowing in concentration. "This is strange. The design and the way the information is presented remind me of the clues we found in the mansion."

Maya took the flyer from Jade and examined it closely. "Do you think it's connected to what we went through?"

"I don't know," I admitted. "But it's worth checking out. There might be something more to this event."

We decided to attend the history night together, our curiosity piqued by the mysterious flyer. The thought of encountering another layer of our past adventures was both thrilling and unnerving.

Jade

The following Saturday evening, we arrived at the historical society's old building. It was a grand, Victorian-era structure that seemed to exude a sense of history and mystery. The air was cool, and the wind rustled through the trees surrounding the building.

Inside, the event was already in full swing. The room was filled with people chatting quietly and sipping on refreshments. The walls were adorned with old photographs and artifacts related to the town's history.

As we mingled and observed, we noticed a display featuring the very mansion we had explored. The display contained photographs and newspaper clippings about its construction, its original owners, and various events that had taken place over the years.

Something about the display felt oddly familiar. I couldn't shake the feeling that there was more to this event than met the eye.

Maya

While Jade and Ethan examined the display, I wandered to a side room where a series of old maps were spread out on tables. I noticed a small group gathered around one of the maps, discussing something animatedly.

I approached them and overheard snippets of their conversation. They were talking about a hidden part of the town's history-something about a series of underground tunnels that had been discovered years ago but had since been sealed off.

The mention of hidden tunnels immediately caught my attention. Could this be related to the mansion and the strange occurrences we had experienced?

I decided to join the conversation. "Hi, I couldn't help but overhear. Are you talking about the old tunnels?"

One of the individuals, a historian named Dr. Jenkins, looked up with interest. "Yes, we're discussing the old tunnels that were discovered a few decades ago. They were thought to be part of an old network used during the town's early days."

I shared our recent experiences with Dr. Jenkins, and he listened with keen interest. "It's fascinating," he said. "These tunnels have always been shrouded in mystery. There are rumors that they connect to various historical sites around town."

Ethan

As Maya spoke with Dr. Jenkins, Jade and I continued to explore the main room. We found ourselves drawn to a large, old ledger displayed under glass. The ledger contained records of various events and transactions related to the mansion.

There was one entry that caught my eye-a notation about an unexplained incident involving a missing person and a cryptic message left behind. The message was eerily similar to some of the cryptic clues we had encountered.

Jade joined me as I examined the ledger. "Look at this," I said, pointing to the entry. "This could be another piece of the puzzle."

Jade nodded, her expression thoughtful. "It's clear that there's more to this story. We need to find out more about these tunnels and how they might be connected to everything we've experienced."

Jade

We regrouped with Maya and Dr. Jenkins, sharing what we had learned. Dr. Jenkins seemed intrigued by our findings and offered to help us investigate further.

"I can arrange a tour of the old tunnels," he said. "It might provide some insight into their history and any connections to the mansion."

The offer was too good to pass up. We agreed to join Dr. Jenkins on the tour, eager to uncover more about the mysterious tunnels and their potential link to our recent experiences.

As we left the historical society, the excitement of the investigation rekindled the thrill we had felt during our previous adventure. The sense of mystery and anticipation was palpable, and we were ready to dive into this new chapter of our journey.

Chapter 16

Jade

The following week, Dr. Jenkins arranged for us to visit the old tunnels. The anticipation was a mix of excitement and trepidation as we approached the entrance to the subterranean passages. The area was located on the outskirts of town, an overgrown path leading to a heavy iron door partially hidden by ivy.

The door creaked as it was pushed open, revealing a dimly lit staircase descending into the darkness. The air was musty, and the temperature dropped noticeably as we descended. I glanced at Ethan and Maya, their faces reflecting a mix of curiosity and apprehension.

"Are you ready?" Dr. Jenkins asked, holding up a flashlight. "These tunnels have been closed off for years, so be prepared for anything."

We nodded and followed him down the staircase, the narrow passageways opening up into a network of dark, stone tunnels. The walls were lined with old, moss-covered bricks, and the air was filled with the scent of damp earth.

Maya

As we ventured deeper into the tunnels, the sense of unease grew. The walls seemed to close in on us, and the only sound was the echo of our footsteps. We used the flashlight to illuminate our path, casting eerie shadows on the walls.

Dr. Jenkins led us through a series of twists and turns, explaining the history of the tunnels as we walked. "These tunnels were used for various purposes over the years," he said. "They were originally built for transportation and storage, but there were rumors of secret activities taking place here."

The mention of secret activities piqued my interest. "What kind of activities?" I asked.

Dr. Jenkins shrugged. "There are various theories. Some believe that the tunnels were used for smuggling or even as a hideout during periods of unrest. However, the specifics remain a mystery."

As we continued, I noticed a faint glimmer in the distance. I nudged Jade and Ethan, pointing it out. "Do you see that? It looks like something is reflecting the light."

Ethan

We approached the glimmer cautiously, the sound of dripping water echoing through the tunnels. As we rounded a corner, we found ourselves in a large, cavernous room. The walls were covered in old, faded symbols and drawings, and in the center of the room was a pedestal with a small, ornate box resting on it.

The box was intricately decorated with strange patterns and symbols that seemed familiar. My heart raced as I approached the pedestal. "This looks like something from the mansion," I said. "The symbols are similar."

Dr. Jenkins examined the box closely, his expression a mix of awe and curiosity. "This is remarkable. It appears to be an artifact of significant historical value."

Jade stepped closer to the pedestal, her eyes fixed on the box. "Could this be connected to the mansion and the mystery we uncovered?"

Dr. Jenkins nodded thoughtfully. "It's possible. The tunnels and the mansion may have been linked in some way. We need to investigate further."

Jade

Dr. Jenkins carefully opened the box, revealing an old, leather-bound journal inside. The journal was worn but still legible, its pages filled with handwritten notes and sketches.

Jade's fingers trembled slightly as she picked up the journal. "This looks like it could contain crucial information. We need to examine it closely."

We gathered around the pedestal, carefully turning the pages of the journal. The entries detailed various experiments and observations related to the supernatural. There were references to rituals, symbols, and unexplained phenomena that mirrored some of the experiences we had encountered.

One entry stood out. It mentioned a powerful artifact hidden within the mansion, said to hold great influence over the supernatural forces we had faced.

"This could be what we were looking for," Ethan said. "The artifact might be key to understanding the full extent of the mansion's mysteries."

Maya

We spent the next hour studying the journal, piecing together its contents and trying to make sense of the information. The more we read, the clearer it became that the journal was connected to our previous adventure.

"There's a reference to a hidden chamber within the mansion," Maya noted. "It seems like the artifact is connected to this chamber."

Dr. Jenkins took careful notes, documenting our findings and the significance of the journal. "This is incredible," he said. "We need to share this information with the historical society and continue our investigation."

As we prepared to leave the tunnels, the excitement of discovery was tempered by the realization that our adventure was far from over. The journal had opened up new questions and possibilities, and we were eager to uncover the full extent of the mansion's secrets.

Back on the surface, we thanked Dr. Jenkins for his assistance and promised to keep him updated on our progress. The journal was now in our possession, and we were determined to delve deeper into its contents and uncover the truth behind the mysterious artifact.

As we headed back to school, the sense of thrill and anticipation was renewed. The shadows of the past were calling us once more, and we were ready to face whatever challenges lay ahead.

Chapter 17

M aya

The next day at school was buzzing with excitement. Word had spread quickly about the historical society's event and our discovery of the journal. We couldn't help but discuss our findings in every spare moment.

During lunch, Jade, Ethan, and I sat together at our usual table in the cafeteria. The conversation flowed easily, a mixture of excitement and nerves.

"I can't believe how detailed the journal was," Jade said, taking a bite of her sandwich. "It's like we've uncovered a whole new layer to the mystery."

"I know," Ethan agreed, sipping his drink. "It makes me wonder what else we might find. The hidden chamber mentioned in the journal could be the key to everything."

Maya leaned forward, her expression thoughtful. "We need to figure out where this hidden chamber is. It might be connected to the artifact and whatever else is going on."

Just then, Laura, one of our friends, approached our table. "Hey, I heard you guys found something incredible at the historical society. What's the scoop?"

Jade and I exchanged a glance before Jade spoke up. "Yeah, we found an old journal that seems to be connected to the mansion and some of the things we experienced."

Laura's eyes widened with interest. "That sounds amazing! I'd love to hear more about it."

We spent a few minutes sharing the basic details with Laura, who listened intently. Her enthusiasm was contagious, and we felt a renewed sense of purpose.

Jade

Later that afternoon, Ethan and I had a free period and decided to head to the library to review the journal's contents. We found a quiet corner and spread out the journal on a table.

"I've been thinking," Ethan said, flipping through the pages. "The references to the hidden chamber are intriguing. But where exactly could it be?"

"I'm not sure," I replied. "But we need to analyze the symbols and clues from the journal. They might point us in the right direction."

We pored over the journal, comparing the symbols to the ones we had seen in the mansion and the tunnels. The more we studied, the more connections we found.

As we were deep in thought, Mr. Thompson, our history teacher, walked by and noticed us. "You two look very focused. What are you working on?"

Ethan glanced up, slightly embarrassed. "We're just looking into some historical documents we found. It's related to a project we're working on."

Mr. Thompson nodded, intrigued. "That sounds interesting. If you need any help with your research, feel free to ask."

We thanked him for his offer and continued our work, grateful for his support. The pieces of the puzzle were slowly coming together, and we were determined to uncover the full story.

Ethan

As evening approached, Jade and I decided to take a break from the research and catch up with Maya. We met her at the park, a favorite hangout spot where we could relax and talk freely.

"Hey, Maya," Jade greeted her with a hug. "How's it going?"

Maya smiled. "Hey! I've been thinking about the journal. There's so much to process. I'm excited but also a little overwhelmed."

We sat on a bench, and Jade and I filled Maya in on our progress. Maya listened attentively, nodding along as we discussed the connections we had found.

"I think we're on the right track," Maya said. "But we need to be careful. We don't know what we might uncover next."

We talked for a while longer, discussing our plans and sharing our thoughts. The sense of camaraderie among us was strong, and it was reassuring to know we had each other's support.

Jade

That night, Ethan and I met up at the library to continue our research. We were determined to make progress on deciphering the symbols and clues from the journal.

As we worked, Ethan brought up an idea. "What if we tried to map out the mansion and the tunnels based on the clues? It might help us locate the hidden chamber."

"That's a good idea," I agreed. "We can use the journal's information to create a detailed map and see if it reveals any patterns."

We spent hours drawing out a map and cross-referencing it with the journal's symbols. The process was meticulous, but it felt like we were making tangible progress.

Around midnight, we finally decided to call it a night. "We're getting closer," Ethan said, stretching. "I can feel it."

I nodded, feeling a mix of exhaustion and excitement. "Definitely. Let's keep at it."

As we packed up our things, I couldn't help but feel a sense of anticipation for what lay ahead. The journey was far from over, and the thrill of discovery kept us motivated.

Chapter 18

Jade

The following day, our excitement was palpable as we arrived at school. The mystery of the hidden chamber and the journal was consuming our thoughts, and we couldn't wait to continue our investigation.

During lunch, we gathered in our usual spot, eager to discuss our progress. Maya and Ethan were already seated when I joined them.

"Morning, guys!" I said, sliding into my seat. "How's the research coming along?"

Maya looked up from her notebook, her eyes bright. "We've made some progress. The symbols from the journal seem to be pointing us towards a specific part of the mansion."

"That's great!" Ethan chimed in. "We've been mapping out the symbols and trying to match them with the mansion's layout. It's like piecing together a giant puzzle."

As we chatted, Laura and a few other friends joined us. Laura was curious about our ongoing project, and we filled her in on the latest developments. Her enthusiasm was a boost to our morale.

"That sounds like an incredible adventure," Laura said. "If you need any extra help or just someone to bounce ideas off of, let me know."

We appreciated Laura's offer and promised to keep her in the loop. The support from our friends was invaluable, and it made us feel less isolated in our quest.

After lunch, Maya and I headed to the library to meet Ethan and continue our research. The library was a quiet sanctuary where we could focus on our tasks without distraction.

As we worked, Maya and I reviewed the journal and compared its contents with the notes Ethan had taken. We were searching for any additional clues that might lead us to the hidden chamber.

"I've been thinking," Maya said, her brow furrowed in concentration. "What if the hidden chamber isn't just a physical space? It could be a symbolic or metaphorical location."

"That's an interesting thought," I replied. "The journal does have references to rituals and symbols. Maybe the chamber represents a state of mind or a revelation we need to uncover."

Our discussion was interrupted by the arrival of Ethan, who brought a stack of additional research materials. "I found some old blueprints of the mansion," he said. "They might help us with our mapping."

We eagerly examined the blueprints, comparing them to our own sketches and notes. The more we analyzed, the clearer the connections between the symbols and the mansion's layout became.

Jade

Later that evening, Ethan and I decided to take a break and grab a coffee at a local café. The atmosphere was relaxed, and it gave us a chance to talk about our progress in a more informal setting.

"I think we're getting closer to something big," Ethan said, stirring his coffee. "The blueprints and the journal are giving us a clearer picture of the mansion's layout."

"I agree," I said, taking a sip of my drink. "But we still need to be cautious. There could be unexpected challenges ahead."

Ethan nodded thoughtfully. "Definitely. We've come a long way, but we need to stay focused and keep our wits about us."

As we chatted, Ethan brought up an idea. "What if we tested some of the symbols and rituals mentioned in the journal? It might help us understand their significance and how they relate to the hidden chamber."

"That's a good idea," I said. "We should consider trying out some of the rituals or symbols to see if they trigger any reactions or reveal new information."

We finished our coffee and headed back to our respective homes, the excitement of our discovery fueling our determination.

Ethan

The next day at school, we reconvened in the library to discuss our findings and plan our next steps. The sense of anticipation was evident in the air.

"I think we should start with the rituals mentioned in the journal," Jade suggested. "Testing them could provide us with valuable insights."

Maya nodded in agreement. "I'll start preparing the materials we need. We can meet after school to test the rituals."

Ethan and I agreed to help with the preparations. We spent the afternoon gathering the necessary items and organizing our research.

As we wrapped up our preparations, Maya looked at us with a mixture of excitement and apprehension. "I'm really looking forward to seeing what we uncover. But let's remember to stay safe and be prepared for anything."

We all agreed, and with a final nod, we parted ways to get ready for our evening investigation. The thrill of discovery was heightened by the anticipation of what lay ahead.

Chapter 19

Maya

The evening had finally arrived. We had spent the day preparing for the ritual, and now it was time to put our plans into action. We met at the mansion, where the air was thick with anticipation.

The mansion's old, creaky doors seemed to groan as we pushed them open. Inside, the atmosphere was eerie, but the excitement of our mission kept us focused. We gathered in the study where we had previously discovered the journal.

"I've set up everything we need for the ritual," I said, laying out the materials on the large wooden table. "We should follow the instructions from the journal closely."

The others nodded in agreement. We had spent hours researching the ritual, making sure we understood every step. Now, it was time to test it.

Jade

I glanced around the room, taking in the dusty shelves and the flickering light of the candles we had placed around the table. The room felt charged with energy, and I could sense the weight of the history surrounding us.

"Let's start with the symbols," I said, picking up a piece of chalk and drawing the intricate patterns described in the journal on the floor. "We need to get this right."

As I worked, I could feel the tension in the room growing. Maya and Ethan prepared the other elements of the ritual, arranging them meticulously. We had made sure to follow every detail from the journal.

Once the symbols were in place and everything was set, we gathered in the center of the room. Ethan took out the journal and began reading the incantation aloud, his voice steady but with an undertone of nervousness.

Ethan

The room was dimly lit by the candles, casting long shadows on the walls. The symbols on the floor seemed to pulse with a faint, otherworldly glow. I read the incantation from the journal, my heart pounding with each word.

The atmosphere was thick with anticipation. As I recited the final words, I felt a sudden chill in the air. The temperature dropped noticeably, and a faint breeze seemed to sweep through the room.

"Did you feel that?" I asked, glancing at Maya and Jade. Their faces mirrored my own unease.

Maya nodded, her eyes wide. "Yes, something's definitely happening."

As the final words of the incantation left my lips, the symbols on the floor began to shimmer. The room was filled with a soft, eerie light, and the shadows on the walls seemed to dance.

Maya

I watched in awe as the symbols on the floor glowed brighter. The atmosphere was electric, and I could feel the energy in the room shifting. The faint light illuminated the journal on the table, and it seemed to react to the ritual.

Suddenly, the light from the symbols converged into a single beam that illuminated a hidden panel in the wall. The panel was concealed behind a bookcase, its presence revealed only by the ritual's energy.

"Look!" I exclaimed, pointing to the illuminated panel. "That must be the hidden chamber mentioned in the journal!"

Jade and Ethan moved quickly, pulling the bookcase aside to reveal the hidden panel. With a creak, the panel slid open, revealing a dark passageway.

Jade

The passageway was narrow and shrouded in darkness, but the beam of light from the ritual provided some illumination. My excitement was palpable as I peered into the unknown.

"Shall we?" I asked, looking at Ethan and Maya. "This is what we've been working towards."

We nodded in agreement and carefully made our way into the passageway. The air was musty and cool, and the walls of the tunnel were lined with old, faded symbols similar to those we had seen earlier.

As we ventured deeper, the passageway seemed to stretch on endlessly. The sense of anticipation was almost overwhelming.

Ethan

The tunnel seemed to wind and twist, but we followed the direction indicated by the glowing symbols. The passage was narrow, and the air was thick with dust and the scent of old, forgotten things.

"There must be something significant at the end of this tunnel," I said, trying to steady my nerves. "Let's keep moving."

We pressed on, the soft light from our flashlights cutting through the darkness. The tunnel eventually opened up into a large chamber. The walls of the chamber were adorned with intricate carvings and symbols, some of which matched those from the journal.

In the center of the chamber stood a pedestal with an ornate box, similar to the one we had seen in the tunnels. The box was covered in dust but otherwise intact.

Maya

We approached the pedestal with a mix of excitement and trepidation. The chamber was filled with an air of ancient mystery, and the pedestal seemed to beckon us.

"This must be it," I said, reaching out to examine the box. "The artifact mentioned in the journal could be inside."

Jade and Ethan stood by as I carefully opened the box. Inside, we found a small, intricately crafted artifact, its surface covered in the same symbols we had seen throughout our investigation.

The artifact seemed to glow softly, and a sense of awe washed over us. We had uncovered a piece of the mystery that had eluded us for so long.

Chapter 20

Maya

The artifact rested in my hands, its surface cool and smooth despite the warmth of the chamber. The intricate symbols carved into it seemed to shift in the candlelight, giving the illusion that the patterns were alive. The object felt heavy with significance, a weight that went beyond its physical properties.

Jade and Ethan hovered nearby, their expressions a mix of awe and curiosity. Jade's eyes were fixed on the artifact, her usual confident demeanor replaced by a palpable sense of wonder. Ethan, ever the methodical one, had already started flipping through the pages of the journal again, searching for any hints about the artifact's purpose.

"This is incredible," Jade said softly, breaking the silence. "We've found something that's been hidden for centuries."

"I know," I replied, turning the artifact over in my hands. "But what exactly does it unlock? The journal mentioned a key, but it didn't specify what it's supposed to open."

Ethan adjusted his glasses and glanced up from the journal. "Let's cross-reference the symbols on the artifact with the ones we've seen in the journal and the mansion. There might be a pattern or a clue that we've missed."

We set up our makeshift research station in the center of the chamber. The large wooden table was covered in notes, sketches, and the now-familiar journal. I carefully placed the artifact on the table and joined Ethan and Jade in examining the symbols.

Ethan

As Maya and Jade focused on the artifact, I turned my attention back to the journal. The entries about the hidden chamber were detailed, but they were also filled with obscure references and symbolic language. It was clear that understanding the artifact was crucial to solving the mystery, but we needed more context.

"Let's look at the sketches in the journal," I suggested. "There are several pages with detailed drawings of symbols and diagrams. We need to compare them with the artifact's carvings."

I pulled out a few pages and laid them side by side with the artifact. The symbols on the artifact were intricate and interlocking, resembling a complex puzzle. Some of the symbols matched those found in the journal, but others were unique.

"This is definitely a key," I said, tracing one of the symbols with my finger. "But the key's purpose isn't immediately clear. We need to figure out how it fits into the overall mystery."

Jade, meanwhile, was photographing the artifact from every angle, capturing its details for later analysis. "I'm documenting everything," she said. "We might find more clues when we review the images later."

Hours passed as we meticulously compared the artifact's symbols with the journal's diagrams. The chamber's atmosphere was filled with the soft rustling of pages and the occasional murmur of discussion. The sense of urgency was palpable; we were on the brink of uncovering something significant, and every detail mattered.

Maya

The clock on the wall ticked away the hours as we worked. Despite our best efforts, the full meaning of the artifact remained elusive. We had managed to identify some of the symbols, but the connections were still unclear.

"I think we need to take a step back," I said, feeling the weight of exhaustion settling in. "We've been at this for hours, and our brains are probably fried."

Jade and Ethan nodded in agreement. "Let's pack up for the night," Jade suggested. "We can review our findings tomorrow with fresh eyes."

We carefully wrapped up the artifact and the journal, ensuring that everything was stored securely. As we left the chamber, the weight of the artifact seemed to linger, a constant reminder of the mystery that lay ahead.

Ethan

The next morning, we reconvened at the library, eager to continue our research. The artifact was carefully placed on a table, and the journal lay open beside it. We had decided to start our analysis anew, focusing on the connections we had previously missed.

"I've been thinking," Maya said, as we settled into our work. "What if the artifact's purpose is related to something in the mansion itself? Maybe it's not just a key, but a tool that interacts with the mansion's features."

"That's a good point," I replied. "The mansion is full of hidden mechanisms and secret rooms. If the artifact is a key, it might interact with one of those features."

Jade, who had been reviewing the photographs she took of the artifact, nodded. "We should map out the mansion again, paying close attention to any areas we might have missed. There might be hidden compartments or mechanisms that the artifact interacts with."

We spent the morning reviewing our notes and reexamining the mansion's blueprints. The task was both exciting and challenging, as we tried to piece together the artifact's role in the larger mystery.

Maya

By early afternoon, we had created a detailed map of the mansion, highlighting the areas we had already explored and marking potential locations for further investigation. The artifact was at the center of our focus, and we were determined to uncover its secrets.

"Let's start with the areas we've identified as potential locations for hidden mechanisms," I suggested. "We need to test the artifact and see if it interacts with any of these spots."

We chose a few locations to investigate, including a large, ornate mirror in the mansion's grand hall and a series of old cabinets in the library. As we approached each location, we carefully examined them for any signs of hidden compartments or mechanisms.

Ethan

Our first stop was the grand hall, where the large mirror stood in a place of prominence. The mirror's frame was adorned with elaborate carvings that matched some of the symbols on the artifact.

"This might be the place,' I said, examining the mirror's frame. "Let's see if the artifact fits or interacts with it in any way."

We carefully approached the mirror, holding the artifact up to the carvings. To our disappointment, there was no immediate reaction. We spent several minutes examining the mirror, but it remained unchanged.

"We might need to try a different approach," Maya said, clearly frustrated. "Let's move on to the next location."

We continued our investigation, trying different methods to interact with the artifact and the mansion's features. Despite our best efforts, the artifact's purpose remained a mystery.

Maya

As the day drew to a close, we regrouped in the library to discuss our findings. The sense of frustration was palpable, but we were determined to continue our search.

"We've covered a lot of ground today," Jade said, looking at the notes and maps scattered across the table. "But we still don't know what the artifact unlocks."

"I think we need to take a step back and reassess," I said. "There must be something we're missing. Maybe the artifact's purpose is more symbolic than we originally thought."

Ethan and Jade agreed, and we decided to review our research again. The artifact's mystery was far from solved, but we were more determined than ever to uncover its secrets.

As we packed up for the night, the artifact remained at the forefront of our minds. We were on the brink of something significant, and we knew that the answers we sought were just within reach.

Chapter 21

Ethan

The morning sun filtered through the library's windows, casting a warm glow over our research table. We had spent the previous evening poring over our notes, trying to find a breakthrough. The artifact was carefully positioned in the center, its surface gleaming under the library lights.

Maya and Jade arrived early, their faces reflecting the exhaustion and determination we all felt. We greeted each other with a nod, ready to continue our search.

"Morning," Maya said, her voice steady despite the weariness in her eyes. "What's our plan for today?"

"I think we should revisit the mansion," I suggested, picking up the journal. "We need to re-examine the areas we previously explored and look for any additional clues. The artifact might interact with something we missed."

Jade agreed, her eyes scanning the journal's pages. "We should also consider any historical records or architectural details that could provide more context about the mansion's design and hidden features."

We spent the next hour gathering our research materials and preparing for another day of investigation. The anticipation was almost tangible as we made our way back to the mansion, each of us brimming with renewed energy and hope.

Maya

Arriving at the mansion, the grand building loomed before us, its dark windows reflecting the morning light. The mansion felt different today, as if it were holding its breath, waiting for us to uncover its secrets.

We headed straight to the grand hall where the mirror stood. Despite our previous unsuccessful attempts, we were determined to give it another try.

"Let's start here again," I said, addressing Ethan and Jade. "We need to be thorough and methodical. There might be a small detail we overlooked."

We examined the mirror's frame and the surrounding area with renewed focus. Ethan held the artifact up to the carvings, while Jade and I scrutinized every inch of the mirror and its surroundings.

After several minutes of careful inspection, Jade noticed something peculiar. "Look at this," she said, pointing to a small indentation in the mirror's frame that we hadn't seen before. "It's almost as if something was meant to fit here."

Ethan moved closer, his eyes narrowing. "It matches the shape of one of the symbols on the artifact. Maybe this is the key to unlocking the mechanism."

With a mixture of excitement and caution, I positioned the artifact near the indentation. As I aligned it with the symbol, there was a faint click. The mirror's frame shifted slightly, revealing a hidden compartment behind it.

Ethan

The hidden compartment was dark and dusty, but there was something intriguing about it. I carefully reached inside, feeling for any objects or mechanisms. My fingers brushed against something cold and metallic.

"I think there's something in here," I said, pulling out a small, ornate box. The box was covered in similar symbols to those on the artifact, and it seemed to pulse with a faint, eerie light.

Maya and Jade gathered around as I placed the box on the floor. The anticipation was palpable as we examined it closely.

"This box might be related to the artifact," Maya said, her eyes wide with excitement. "Let's open it and see what's inside."

I carefully opened the box, revealing an array of ancient documents, maps, and additional artifacts. Each item was carefully preserved, and the symbols on them matched those on the artifact and the mansion's features.

Maya

Among the documents and artifacts, one item stood out—a detailed map of the mansion with additional markings and annotations. It seemed to offer a new perspective on the mansion's layout.

"This map could be the key to understanding the artifact's purpose," I said, studying the map closely. "It shows areas we haven't explored yet and provides clues about hidden rooms and mechanisms."

Jade examined the documents, her eyes scanning the text. "There are also notes about specific rituals and symbols. We might find

more information about how the artifact interacts with the mansion."

We spent the next few hours meticulously analyzing the documents and the new map. Each piece of information added to our
growing understanding of the mansion's mysteries.

Ethan

As the day wore on, we made significant progress. The new map
and documents revealed several previously unknown features of
the mansion. We identified key areas that needed further exploration and began to formulate a plan for our next steps.

"This is incredible," Jade said, looking up from the documents.
"We've uncovered more clues than we expected."

"We're getting closer to solving the mystery," I agreed. "But we
still have a lot of work ahead of us."

We decided to focus on one of the newly identified areas—the
mansion's west wing, which appeared to have several hidden rooms
and passages. The artifacts and documents suggested that this part
of the mansion might hold the final piece of the puzzle.

Maya

As we prepared to explore the west wing, I felt a mix of excitement
and nervousness. The mansion's mysteries were slowly unraveling,
but there were still many unanswered questions.

"We need to be careful," I said, addressing Ethan and Jade. "The
mansion has already proven to be full of surprises. Let's stick together and stay alert."

We made our way to the west wing, the air thick with anticipation.
The old wooden doors creaked as we pushed them open, revealing
a series of dusty, dimly lit rooms.

Our exploration revealed several intriguing features—hidden compartments, old furniture covered in dust, and faint symbols carved into the walls. Each discovery brought us closer to understanding the artifact and the mansion's secrets.

Ethan

As we delved deeper into the west wing, we encountered a series of old, ornate doors, each adorned with intricate carvings. One of the doors seemed to be slightly ajar, revealing a glimpse of a room beyond.

"This door looks promising," I said, pushing it open carefully. The room inside was filled with old, weathered furniture and shelves lined with dusty books.

In the center of the room stood a large, ornate chest, its surface covered in more symbols. It looked similar to the box we had found earlier.

"This might be another key to understanding the artifact," Maya said, her eyes lighting up. "Let's open it and see what's inside."

We approached the chest with a mix of excitement and caution. As I unlocked it, the lid creaked open, revealing a collection of old manuscripts and additional artifacts. The manuscripts were filled with more information about the mansion's history and the role of the artifact.

Maya

The new manuscripts provided valuable insights into the mansion's past and the purpose of the artifact. The documents described a series of rituals and symbols that were used to protect and conceal important secrets.

"This is amazing," I said, scanning the manuscripts. "We're learning so much about the mansion's history and the artifact's role in it."

Jade and Ethan agreed, their faces reflecting the same sense of wonder and accomplishment. We had made significant progress, but there was still much to uncover.

As the sun set and we prepared to leave the mansion, I felt a sense of satisfaction. We had uncovered new clues and made substantial progress in solving the mystery. The artifact's secrets were slowly being revealed, and the mansion's hidden past was coming to light.

Chapter 22

Maya

There's a weight in my chest as we step back into the mansion. It's heavy with the unknown, the fear that whatever we find might change everything. My hands are trembling slightly, and I can't tell if it's from excitement or dread. The mansion isn't just a mystery anymore; it's a puzzle that seems to be leading us deeper into something I'm not sure I want to uncover.

Ethan and Jade are beside me, their faces tense. Ethan's usually so composed, but I can see the flicker of uncertainty in his eyes. Jade, on the other hand, is biting her lip, a sure sign that she's nervous. She's been that way ever since we found the manuscripts. I don't blame her. There's something off about this place, something that feels like it's waiting for us to make the wrong move.

I catch Ethan's eye as we approach the hidden panel in the wall. His expression softens just a bit, and he nods. "We've got this," he says, but his voice doesn't quite reach the confidence I know he's trying to project. I try to smile back, but it feels tight on my face.

We place the artifact against the wall, the metal cool and ancient in my hands. For a moment, nothing happens, and I feel a rush of panic. What if we're wrong? But then, there's a faint click, and the panel begins to shift. The hidden passage yawns open before us, dark and foreboding.

Jade lets out a breath she's been holding, her relief palpable. "This is it," she murmurs, more to herself than to us. "We're really doing this."

I swallow hard and step into the passage first, the air cool and musty as it wraps around me like a shroud. The walls are lined with faded wallpaper, long-forgotten patterns barely visible under the grime. The passage feels alive somehow, as if it's been waiting for someone to walk its length after all these years.

Ethan

Maya's courage never ceases to amaze me. She's always the first to step into the unknown, even when she's scared. I can see it in the way her shoulders tense up, in how she glances back at us to make sure we're following. She doesn't have to say it; I know she's terrified, but she pushes through it anyway. That's why I'm right behind her, because if she's willing to face whatever this mansion is hiding, then so am I.

Jade's quiet as she trails behind, her eyes darting around like she's waiting for something to jump out at us. She's always been the cautious one, the thinker, but I know she's just as determined as Maya to see this through. We all are. There's no turning back now.

The passage twists and turns, each step echoing in the silence. It's unsettling, this quiet. I'm used to hearing something—birds, the wind, anything—but down here, there's nothing. Just the sound of our breathing and the occasional creak of the floorboards above. It's enough to make my skin crawl.

We come across the first door, and it's like a punch to the gut. The symbols carved into it match the ones on the artifact, and I can feel a rush of adrenaline. We're on the right track, but there's also a part of me that wishes we weren't. There's something unnatural about this place, something that feels... wrong.

"This door," I say, more to myself than to the others. "It's connected to the artifact somehow." My hand hovers over the keyhole, hesitating. What if this door opens to something we're not ready for?

But there's no room for hesitation. We've come too far. I try the artifact, hoping for another click, another reveal. But the door doesn't budge. It's frustrating, like we're missing a piece of the puzzle. I move to the next door, pushing it open carefully. The room inside is dark, but the musty smell of old books and dust fills my senses. I can see the outlines of furniture and shelves, relics of a time long past.

"This room looks promising," Maya says, and there's a note of hope in her voice that I haven't heard in days. She steps inside, and I follow, watching as she runs her fingers over the dusty surfaces.

Maya

The room feels ancient, like stepping back into a different time. The air is thick with dust, and I can practically taste the age in every breath. But there's something else here, something that makes my heart race. Maybe it's the sheer amount of history packed into this room, or maybe it's just the idea that we're finally getting somewhere.

My hands shake as I pick up an old map, the paper so brittle it feels like it might crumble under my touch. The markings are faded, but I can still make out the layout of the mansion. There are rooms and passages we haven't even begun to explore, hidden depths that this map hints at.

"This map... it shows more," I say, spreading it out on the table. The lines and symbols blur in my vision for a moment, and I blink rapidly, trying to focus. "There are more rooms, more passages. We haven't seen half of what's down there."

Jade steps closer, her face drawn tight with concentration. "Look at this," she says, pointing to a specific area. "This one says 'ritual room.' It's deeper underground, almost at the very bottom."

I meet her gaze, and for a second, the fear I've been pushing down surges up, threatening to choke me. A ritual room? The thought sends a shiver down my spine. What kind of rituals could they have been performing here? And why is it hidden so deep beneath the mansion?

Ethan's voice breaks through my thoughts. "If that room is as important as it sounds, we need to find it. It might be the key to understanding what this place really is." He's always been the one to ground us, to bring us back to the task at hand.

I nod, but the anxiety gnaws at me. The mansion feels like a living thing, watching us, waiting. The air seems thicker now, as if the walls themselves are holding their breath, anticipating what we'll find.

Ethan

The tunnels feel even more oppressive now, the air damp and heavy as we descend deeper into the mansion's bowels. Every step feels like we're walking into something we can't come back from. I can tell Maya's on edge, and Jade hasn't said a word since we left the room. The weight of the mansion's history is pressing down on us, more than it ever has before.

As we approach what we think is the ritual room, the atmosphere shifts. It's colder, the kind of cold that seeps into your bones, that makes your breath fog in front of you. I can feel something watching us, something that's been here long before we ever stepped foot inside this place.

"This is it," Maya whispers, her voice trembling just a bit. "We're here."

The door looms in front of us, covered in those same ancient symbols, but there's something different about these. They're not just carvings; they seem to pulse with energy, like they're alive.

I push the door open, and we step into the room. The first thing that hits me is the smell—damp earth, mixed with something metallic, like old blood. The walls are covered in strange, unholy symbols, and in the center of the room is a stone altar, stained dark with something I don't want to think about.

"This place..." Jade's voice is barely a whisper. "What happened here?"

Maya

The room is suffocating, the air thick with a sense of dread. The altar in the center of the room draws my gaze, and I can't look away. The dark stains on the stone tell a story I don't want to know. My heart is pounding so hard it feels like it's going to burst out of my chest.

I take a step forward, compelled by something I don't understand. The symbols on the walls seem to twist and writhe in the dim light, and for a moment, I feel dizzy. I can't tell if it's real or just my mind playing tricks on me.

"This is where it happened," I say, my voice barely audible. "Whatever... whoever was here, this is where it all went wrong."

Ethan is by my side, his hand on my arm steadying me. "We need to figure out what they were doing here," he says, though I can hear the unease in his voice. He's trying to stay strong, but this place is getting to him too.

We begin to search the room, but every movement feels like it's being watched. The shadows seem to move on their own, and the silence is deafening. My hands are shaking as I open a small, ornate chest near the altar. Inside, there's a collection of old manuscripts and a small, intricate box.

I lift the box out, and it's heavier than I expected. The designs on it are similar to those on the artifact, and as I turn it over in my hands, I feel a surge of dread.

"This box... it's connected to the artifact," I say, my voice trembling. "This could be the key to everything."

Jade looks at me, her eyes wide with fear and something else—hope, maybe. "Open it," she says, her voice barely above a whisper.

I hesitate for a moment, but then I feel a strange compulsion, like the box is urging me to open it. My fingers find the small latch, and with a deep breath, I flip it open. The lid creaks, the sound loud in the oppressive silence of the room.

Inside the box is a small, ornate key, and beneath it, a folded piece of parchment. My heart skips a beat as I pick up the key, its surface cool and smooth. There's something ancient about it, something that feels like it holds the weight of centuries.

Ethan steps closer, his eyes fixed on the key. "That must be what we've been looking for," he says, his voice low and tense. "But what does it open?"

Jade carefully unfolds the parchment, her brow furrowing as she reads. "It's some kind of ritual instructions," she says, her voice barely audible. "But it's in a language I don't recognize. This must have been used with the artifact for something... something power-ful."

The room seems to pulse with energy, as if it's reacting to the discovery. My heart is racing, and I can feel the weight of the key in my hand, heavy with the unknown. This key, this room, the ritual... it's all connected, and it's all leading us toward something we can't fully understand.

"We need to be careful," I say, my voice trembling slightly. "Whatever this key unlocks, it's tied to the mansion's darkest secrets. We have to be sure we're ready before we use it."

But even as I say the words, I know that we're already too deep. The mansion has drawn us in, and there's no turning back now. We have to see this through to the end, whatever that end might be.

Chapter 23

E than

The morning light filters weakly through the dusty windows, casting long shadows across the room. I've barely slept, my mind replaying the events of last night over and over again. The discovery of the key and the ritual instructions has shaken all of us, and the mansion feels even more oppressive, its secrets pressing down on us like a heavy weight.

Jade is already awake, sitting by the window and staring out at the overgrown gardens. Her expression is distant, her thoughts clearly still tangled in the web of mysteries we've uncovered. I can't blame her. None of us expected this place to be so... alive.

I rise quietly, not wanting to disturb Maya, who's finally managed to fall asleep. She's curled up on the couch, the key clutched tightly in her hand even in sleep. It's like she's guarding it, even in her dreams. The sight of her like that makes my chest tighten, a mix of protectiveness and fear twisting together.

Jade glances over as I approach, her eyes questioning. "Did you get any sleep?" she asks softly, careful not to wake Maya.

"Not really," I admit, rubbing a hand over my face. "Too much on my mind."

"Same here." She looks back out the window, her brow furrowed. "This place... it's starting to get to me. I can't shake the feeling that we're being watched."

Her words send a shiver down my spine. I've felt it too, that eerie sensation of unseen eyes tracking our every move. It's like the mansion itself is alive, its walls breathing, its shadows hiding things that shouldn't be there.

"I know," I say, keeping my voice low. "We need to figure out what that key unlocks, but we can't rush into anything. We have to be smart about this."

Jade nods, but I can see the worry in her eyes. "What if we're in over our heads, Ethan? What if this is more than we can handle?"

I don't have an answer for her, but I can't let her see my doubt. "We'll handle it," I say, trying to sound more confident than I feel. "We have to."

Maya stirs on the couch, her fingers tightening around the key as she wakes. She blinks sleepily at us, then sits up, brushing her hair out of her eyes. "Morning," she murmurs, her voice thick with sleep.

"Morning," I reply, offering her a small smile. "How are you feeling?"

She hesitates, her gaze dropping to the key in her hand. "Honestly? I'm scared," she admits, her voice barely above a whisper. "This place... it's like it's alive. And it's pulling us in deeper and deeper."

"We're all scared," I say, sitting down beside her. "But we're in this together. We'll figure it out."

Maya nods, but I can see the fear still lurking in her eyes. "We need to know what this key unlocks," she says, her voice firmer now. "Whatever it is, it's the next piece of the puzzle."

"We'll find it," Jade agrees, though her tone is cautious. "But we need to be careful. The mansion isn't going to make this easy for us."

We spend the morning combing through the mansion, searching for anything that might match the key. The mansion is massive, with countless rooms, hidden doors, and secret passageways, and the task feels overwhelming. But we have no choice. This key is our only lead, and we have to follow it wherever it takes us.

Hours pass, and frustration begins to set in. Every door we try, every lock we examine, is a dead end. The key seems almost taunting, its secrets just out of reach.

By midday, we're all feeling the strain. Maya is pacing, her anxiety evident in every step. Jade is sitting on the floor, her head in her hands. I'm leaning against a wall, trying to think of what we're missing, where we haven't looked yet.

"We're going in circles," Maya says, her voice tinged with frustration. "This isn't getting us anywhere."

"There has to be something we're overlooking," I say, though I'm not sure I believe it. "Something we've missed."

Jade lifts her head, a sudden thought crossing her mind. "What about the attic?" she suggests. "We haven't checked there yet."

The attic. It's the one place we've avoided, partly because it's so difficult to access and partly because of the stories we've heard about it. But if there's anywhere left to check, it's there.

Maya's eyes meet mine, and I can see the determination hardening in them. "Then let's go," she says. "We're not going to find anything standing around down here."

The climb to the attic is steep and treacherous. The staircase is narrow, the wood creaking ominously under our weight. The air grows colder as we ascend, a chill that seems to seep into our bones. By the time we reach the top, the temperature has dropped noticeably, and the atmosphere is thick with dust and shadows.

The attic door is old and weathered, the wood splintered in places. It feels like it hasn't been opened in years, maybe even decades. I take a deep breath, then push the door open with a creak that echoes through the empty space.

The attic is vast, filled with old trunks, broken furniture, and cobwebs that hang like veils in the dim light. The ceiling slopes down sharply, making it feel even more claustrophobic. The only light comes from a single small window at the far end, the glass so dirty that it barely lets in any sunlight.

We step inside, the floorboards creaking underfoot. The air is thick with dust, and the smell of decay lingers in the corners. It's like the attic has been forgotten by time, left to rot away in the darkness.

Maya moves cautiously through the space, her eyes scanning the room. "It's like a time capsule up here," she says, her voice echoing softly. "Everything's been left exactly as it was."

"There's got to be something here," Jade says, her voice tight with tension. "Something that connects to the key."

We start searching the attic, sifting through the piles of junk and forgotten relics. It's slow going, and the dust and darkness make it difficult to see anything clearly. But we push on, driven by the need to find answers.

After what feels like hours, I finally spot something unusual. In the far corner of the attic, partially hidden under a rotting blanket, is a small, ornate chest. It's old, the wood darkened with age, but the intricate carvings on its surface are still visible. And there, in the center of the chest, is a small, oddly shaped keyhole.

"Maya," I call out, my voice sharp with excitement. "Over here!"

She rushes over, followed closely by Jade. I pull the chest out into the open, my hands trembling slightly as I reach for the key. It fits perfectly into the lock, and with a soft click, the chest opens.

Inside is a single object: a small, intricately carved wooden box, no bigger than the palm of my hand. It's beautiful in a way that feels almost otherworldly, the craftsmanship so delicate that it's hard to believe it was made by human hands.

Maya reaches out, her fingers brushing against the smooth surface of the box. "What is it?" she whispers, her voice filled with awe.

"I don't know," I admit, though the sight of it sends a chill down my spine. "But I think we're about to find out."

As we lift the box from the chest, the attic suddenly feels colder, the air growing heavy with a strange, oppressive energy. The walls seem to close in around us, and for a moment, I swear I hear something-a whisper, a voice just on the edge of hearing, calling out from the darkness.

Maya's hand tightens around the box, her expression one of grim determination. "Whatever this is," she says, her voice steady, "it's the key to everything. We're getting closer."

Jade nods, though she looks pale, her eyes wide with fear. "But closer to what?"

I don't have an answer, but as we make our way back down from the attic, the box clutched tightly in Maya's hands, I can't shake the feeling that whatever we've just uncovered, it's something that should have remained hidden.

And as we step back into the mansion's shadowy corridors, I realize that the watchers-the presence we've all felt lurking in the darkness-are closer than ever. Watching, waiting for us to make our next move.

Chapter 24

Jade

The wooden box in Maya's hands feels like it holds the weight of the entire mansion, and the tension among us is almost unbearable. We descend from the attic in silence, the creak of each step down the narrow staircase echoing like a drumbeat. The old wood groans under our weight, and I can feel my heartbeat quicken with each footfall. The air feels thick, almost stifling, as if the mansion itself is holding its breath, waiting for what we'll do next.

Once we're back on the main floor, the oppressive energy we felt in the attic lingers like a heavy cloud. Maya and Ethan exchange a glance, both of them looking as unsettled as I feel. The ornate box, though small, seems to radiate a strange power. It's as if the secrets of this place are finally within our grasp, but at what cost?

"I think we should open it," Maya says, her voice breaking the silence. Her fingers tremble slightly as she runs them over the delicate carvings on the box.

"Here?" Ethan asks, his voice uncertain. He glances around the dimly lit corridor, as if expecting the walls to close in on us at any moment. "Shouldn't we—"

"Wait?" I finish for him, my voice more steady than I feel. "We've waited long enough. Whatever's inside, it might give us the answers we need."

Maya nods, but the hesitation is still there in her eyes. She's always been the brave one, the one to push us forward, but even she seems to sense the gravity of what we're about to do. The box feels like a Pandora's box—one that, once opened, could change everything.

"We need to find somewhere safe," Ethan says, his eyes scanning the corridor. "Somewhere away from... whatever's in this place."

There's a room at the end of the hallway that we haven't explored much—a small parlor, once used as a study, judging by the dusty bookshelves and the old desk pushed against the wall. The furniture is covered with sheets, but it feels less oppressive than the other rooms we've been in. It's quieter here, as if the mansion's malevolent presence doesn't reach this far.

Maya sets the box down on the desk, and we all gather around it, our breaths held in collective anticipation. The carvings on the box seem to dance in the low light, intricate patterns that draw the eye in, making it hard to look away. There's something almost hypnotic about it.

I swallow hard, trying to dispel the unease that's settled in my chest. "Are we ready?" I ask, my voice barely above a whisper.

No one answers, but the tension in the room speaks for itself. Maya takes a deep breath and reaches for the lid, her fingers brushing against the smooth wood. For a moment, everything seems to freeze—time, the air, even our own thoughts.

Then, with a soft click, the lid opens.

Inside, the box is lined with dark velvet, and nestled within is a small, weathered journal. Its cover is cracked and faded, the leather worn smooth from age. A shiver runs through me as I realize just how old this journal must be—how many hands it has passed through, how many secrets it holds.

Maya lifts the journal out of the box with the same reverence one might use to handle a sacred artifact. The air around us seems to grow heavier, charged with the weight of history and the unknown. She carefully opens the journal, revealing pages filled with spidery handwriting, the ink faded but still legible.

"This is it," she whispers, her eyes scanning the first page. "This is what we've been looking for."

Ethan leans in closer, his eyes narrowing as he tries to make out the words. "It's a journal... but whose?"

Maya flips through the pages, her brow furrowed in concentration. "I don't know. But it's talking about the rituals. The key... it's mentioned here."

She starts reading aloud, her voice barely above a murmur. The journal details the life of someone who once lived in this mansion—someone who was deeply involved in the rituals and the dark history that haunts this place. The entries are cryptic, filled with references to "the watchers," "the binding," and a curse that was never lifted.

My heart pounds in my chest as the pieces start to fall into place. The journal is a map, a guide to the twisted past of this mansion. It speaks of sacrifices, of binding spirits to the house, and of a ritual that was never completed—a ritual that was meant to trap something within these walls.

"The watchers..." Maya reads, her voice trembling slightly. "They are bound to the house. They were never meant to leave, but the ritual was incomplete. Now they linger, trapped between worlds."

"Who wrote this?" Ethan asks, his voice low and tense. "Who was involved in these rituals?"

Maya turns to the last page, where the handwriting becomes more erratic, the words scrawled in desperation. "The final entry," she says, her voice shaking. "It says... 'They are watching. Always watching. The key... it must not be used. The ritual cannot be completed. If it is, we are all lost.'"

The words hang in the air, heavy and ominous. The key that we found, the one that led us to this box—it wasn't meant to be used. But for what? What happens if we complete the ritual?

"We need to stop," I say, my voice firm. "We can't go any further. This—this is too dangerous."

But even as I say the words, I know it's too late. We've already opened the box, already taken the first steps down this dark path. And something in this house, something ancient and malevolent, is waiting for us to finish what was started all those years ago.

"We can't just stop," Maya says, her voice laced with a mix of fear and determination. "If we don't finish this, the watchers... whatever they are... they'll never let us leave."

The room feels colder, and I swear I can hear the faintest whisper, like a breath against my ear. We're in too deep now, and there's no turning back.

The journal, the key, the box—they've all led us to this moment. And whatever comes next, we have to face it. Together.

Ethan's hand tightens around mine, and I can see the resolve in his eyes. We don't have a choice. We have to finish this.

Maya closes the journal, the finality of the gesture echoing in the silence of the room. "There's one more thing," she says, her voice quiet. "The ritual... it requires a sacrifice."

The words send a jolt of fear through me, but I don't let go of Ethan's hand. We're in this together, no matter what. The shadows of the mansion press in around us, and I know that the watchers are waiting, their eyes fixed on us.

This is the final test. And we have to be ready.

Chapter 25

Maya

The weight of the journal in my hands feels more like a curse than a guide. Its pages whisper of ancient rituals and dark forces, and the deeper we delve into its contents, the more I realize how far beyond our control this situation has spiraled. Yet, there's no going back. The watchers are waiting, their presence an unspoken threat lingering in the air, and the only way out of this nightmare is forward.

Jade and Ethan stand close, their faces pale in the dim light. The room feels like a cocoon, the shadows thickening around us as if the mansion itself is tightening its grip. There's no escape, no running from the truth we've uncovered. And now, with the knowledge of the ritual, we've awakened something that was better left buried.

"We need to figure out what this sacrifice means," I say, my voice low but steady. I'm trying to sound confident, but inside, I'm trembling. The thought of what the ritual might demand from us is terrifying.

Jade's hand grips Ethan's tightly, their connection a silent reassurance in the face of the unknown. "Sacrifice could mean anything," Jade says, her eyes filled with a mix of fear and determination. "It doesn't necessarily mean... someone's life."

Ethan looks unconvinced, his brow furrowing in thought. "But what if it does? What if... one of us has to...?"

I don't let him finish the sentence. "We're not jumping to conclusions. There has to be another way." My mind races, trying to piece together what we know. "The ritual was never completed. Maybe... maybe it doesn't have to be. If we can find out what went wrong last time, maybe we can reverse it."

Jade nods, a flicker of hope in her eyes. "Maybe we can find a way to unbind the watchers. To set them free without finishing the ritual."

Ethan looks between us, his expression torn. "And if we can't?"

Silence falls over the room, heavy and suffocating. I don't have an answer. None of us do. All we have is the journal, the key, and a creeping sense of dread.

"We'll figure it out," I say, more for my own sake than theirs. "But first, we need to understand exactly what we're dealing with. There might be more clues in the journal."

I flip back through the pages, scanning the entries for anything we might have missed. The handwriting becomes more frantic as the journal progresses, the author clearly becoming more desperate as the ritual drew closer. The words blur together, the language archaic and difficult to decipher, but certain phrases stand out—references to "the binding," "the offering," and "the blood of the chosen."

My breath catches as I read the last phrase. "The blood of the chosen..." I murmur.

"What does that mean?" Ethan asks, leaning closer.

I shake my head, my mind racing. "I don't know. But it's mentioned multiple times. Whoever wrote this... they were afraid. They knew that the ritual required something—someone—but they didn't want to go through with it."

Jade's face pales as she looks at me. "Are you saying that... we might be the 'chosen'?"

I don't answer. I can't. The thought alone is too horrifying to consider, but deep down, I know that it's a possibility we can't ignore.

"There's only one way to find out," I say finally, my voice hardening with resolve. "We need to go back to where this all started. To the ritual site."

Ethan looks at me like I've lost my mind. "You want to go to the heart of the curse?"

"Do we have a choice?" I counter, my eyes locking with his. "The watchers are bound to this place, but we're not. If we can find the site, maybe we can put an end to this once and for all. And if there's a way to do it without the sacrifice... we need to know."

Jade swallows hard, but there's a steely determination in her eyes. "I'm with you. We have to try."

Ethan hesitates for a moment, then nods, his expression grim. "Alright. Let's end this."

We gather our things, and I slip the journal into my backpack, its weight a constant reminder of the danger we're facing. The mansion seems to pulse with energy as we make our way through the darkened halls, the air growing colder with each step. It's as if the house knows what we're planning, and it doesn't like it.

The ritual site, according to the journal, is somewhere beneath the mansion—a hidden chamber accessible only through a secret passage. We've explored almost every inch of this place, but there's one area we've avoided: the cellar. It's a place we've all instinctively steered clear of, the air down there thick with an overwhelming sense of dread.

As we descend the narrow staircase leading to the cellar, the darkness closes in around us, and I can feel my heart pounding in my chest. The steps creak underfoot, and the musty scent of damp earth fills my nostrils. I can barely see a foot in front of me, but I press on, driven by a mixture of fear and determination.

At the bottom of the stairs, the cellar opens up into a wide, low-ceilinged room, the walls lined with shelves filled with dusty bottles and crates. The air is heavy with the scent of decay, and the faintest whisper of something ancient and malevolent seems to linger in the shadows.

"There," Jade whispers, pointing to a section of the wall that looks different from the rest. The bricks are slightly misaligned, the mortar cracked and crumbling. "It has to be behind there."

Ethan steps forward, running his hand along the wall. "There's a draft... It's hollow behind this."

With a deep breath, he starts pushing on the bricks, and slowly, the wall begins to give way. The bricks crumble to the ground, revealing a dark passageway beyond. The air that rushes out is cold, as if it's been sealed away for centuries.

"This is it," I whisper, my voice trembling.

Jade takes my hand, her grip tight. "We're in this together."

Ethan glances back at us, his expression a mix of fear and determination. "Let's finish this."

We step into the passageway, the darkness swallowing us whole. The walls close in around us, and the cold seeps into our bones. The passage twists and turns, leading us deeper beneath the mansion, and the sense of dread grows stronger with each step.

Finally, we reach the end of the passage, and the space opens up into a cavernous chamber. The air is thick with the scent of earth and something far more sinister. In the center of the chamber is an ancient altar, covered in strange symbols that glow faintly in the darkness.

"This is where it happened," I whisper, my voice barely audible. "This is where they tried to bind the watchers."

The altar seems to pulse with a malevolent energy, and I can feel the presence of the watchers all around us, their eyes fixed on us from the shadows. The journal's warnings echo in my mind, and I know that we're standing on the edge of something terrifying and unknown.

But there's no turning back now.

"We need to find a way to undo this," I say, my voice trembling. "We have to..."

Before I can finish, the ground beneath us starts to shake, and the symbols on the altar flare to life, casting an eerie light over the chamber. The watchers are here, their presence a tangible force that presses in on us from all sides.

The ritual has already begun.

Jade screams as the shadows close in around us, and Ethan grabs my hand, pulling me back towards the passage. But the entrance has vanished, the walls closing in, trapping us in the chamber.

The journal's final words echo in my mind: *The key... it must not be used. The ritual cannot be completed. If it is, we are all lost.*

And I realize, with a sinking heart, that we've walked right into the trap.

Chapter 26

Jade

The chamber trembles with a deep, resonant hum, and the symbols on the altar glow with an eerie, pulsating light. My heart races as I try to make sense of the chaos unfolding around us. The shadows seem to move with a life of their own, swirling and coiling like living things. The oppressive energy in the room is almost suffocating, and I can feel a cold sweat forming on the back of my neck.

Ethan's grip on my hand is tight, his knuckles white as he pulls me towards the altar. "We need to stop this," he says, his voice strained. "There has to be something we can do."

The altar's symbols cast distorted shadows on the walls, and I can see the faint outlines of figures moving in the darkness. The watchers are here, their presence almost palpable, a dark and unrelenting force that seems to be closing in on us.

"Look at the symbols," I shout over the noise. "They're reacting to us. Maybe... maybe there's something we can do to disrupt the ritual."

Maya, standing a few feet away, is frantically flipping through the journal, her face pale and drawn. "I'm trying to find anything that might help," she calls out, her voice barely audible over the growing noise. "But it's all so... vague."

Ethan and I make our way to the altar, trying to decipher the glowing symbols. They're intricate and alien, a web of lines and shapes that seem to shift and change as we move. I reach out, my fingers brushing against the surface of the altar, and a jolt of cold energy runs through me.

"Careful!" Maya warns. "We don't know what touching it will do."

I pull my hand back, shaking off the chill that has settled into my bones. "We need to find a way to disrupt the symbols. If we can break the connection, maybe we can stop the ritual."

Ethan looks around the chamber, his eyes scanning the walls for any clue. "There's got to be something here," he says, his voice filled with desperation. "Some kind of mechanism or hidden passage..."

As we search the chamber, the symbols on the altar flare brighter, and the shadows around us grow more aggressive, reaching out with tendrils of darkness that seem to stretch towards us. The air grows colder, and I can see my breath in front of me, a sign of the unnatural chill that has settled over the room.

"We're running out of time," Maya says, her voice trembling. "If we don't figure this out soon..."

Suddenly, a gust of wind sweeps through the chamber, sending papers and debris flying. The wind seems to come from nowhere, its source hidden in the darkness. The gust is strong enough to make us stagger, and I catch sight of something glowing in the corner of the chamber—a faint light that seems to pulse in time with the altar's symbols.

"There!" I shout, pointing to the glowing object. "Maybe that's the key."

We make our way to the corner of the chamber, where the light is coming from. It's an old, ornate box, similar to the one we found in the attic, but much larger. The box is covered in the same symbols as the altar, and it's clear that it's an integral part of the ritual.

Maya examines the box, her eyes wide with recognition. "This looks like the box from the attic," she says. "But it's bigger. It might hold the final piece of the puzzle."

Ethan and I help her open the box, and inside, we find a collection of strange objects—ritual tools, old scrolls, and what appears to be a vial of dark liquid. The vial is labeled with an unfamiliar symbol, and a sense of dread washes over me as I realize what it might contain.

"It's blood," Maya says, her voice barely above a whisper. "This is what they were using for the sacrifice."

I feel a wave of nausea at the thought. The ritual was never meant to be completed, but it's clear that this box contains the elements needed to finish it. The final piece of the puzzle is right in front of us, and the ritual is closer to completion than we thought.

"We need to destroy this," Ethan says firmly. "If we can't stop the ritual, we can at least make sure it can't be completed."

We start to gather the items from the box, trying to find a way to destroy them. The vial of blood is especially disturbing, and I can't shake the feeling that it's the key to finishing the ritual. If we can't get rid of it, there's a good chance that the ritual will proceed, with or without us.

As we work, the chamber's energy grows more chaotic. The shadows seem to writhe and twist, and the symbols on the altar flare brighter, their light becoming almost blinding. The air is filled with an oppressive heat, and I can feel the ritual's power pressing in on us, a force that seems to be fighting back against our attempts to stop it.

Suddenly, a loud crack echoes through the chamber, and the ground beneath us starts to shake violently. The altar's symbols flash with a blinding light, and the shadows around us grow more aggressive, their tendrils reaching out as if trying to pull us into the darkness.

"We need to get out!" Maya shouts. "Now!"

But as we turn to leave, the passage we came through is blocked by a wall of solid darkness. We're trapped, with no way to escape the chamber and the ritual's final stages.

"We're running out of time," Ethan says, his voice filled with panic. "We need to find a way to stop this before it's too late."

I look around the chamber, desperately searching for anything that might help us. The symbols on the altar are glowing fiercely now, their light almost blinding. The shadows are closing in, and I can feel their malevolent presence pressing in on us.

Then, I see it—a small, hidden compartment in the wall, partially obscured by the altar. The compartment is filled with more ritual tools and a large, ornate book. The book is bound in dark leather, and it bears the same symbols as the altar.

"That's it," I say, pointing to the compartment. "We need to get that book. It might hold the key to stopping the ritual."

Ethan and Maya rush to the compartment, pulling out the book and examining it. The cover is covered in ancient symbols, and the pages are filled with detailed diagrams and instructions for the ritual. The final steps are outlined clearly, and it's obvious that we're running out of time.

"We need to destroy this book," Maya says, her voice filled with determination. "It's the last piece of the puzzle."

Ethan nods, his face set in a grim expression. "Let's do it."

We gather the book and the remaining ritual tools, making sure to destroy everything we can. The chamber's energy grows more chaotic, the shadows reaching out with increasing ferocity. The symbols on the altar are almost blinding now, and the pressure in the room is almost unbearable.

With a final, desperate effort, we manage to destroy the book and the ritual tools, the remnants burning brightly in the center of the chamber. The energy in the room seems to shift, and the shadows start to recede, their presence fading as the ritual's power is disrupted.

The ground stops shaking, and the blinding light from the altar fades. The oppressive heat lifts, and the chamber returns to its former state, though it's still filled with a lingering sense of dread.

"We did it," Maya says, her voice filled with exhaustion. "We stopped the ritual."

I look around the chamber, still feeling the weight of what we've been through. The shadows are gone, and the energy in the room is no longer oppressive. But the sense of unease remains, a reminder of the darkness that still lingers.

"We need to get out of here," Ethan says, his voice firm. "We've done what we can."

We make our way back through the passage, the darkness receding as we leave the chamber behind. The mansion still feels oppressive, but there's a sense of relief that we've managed to disrupt the ritual and prevent it from being completed.

As we emerge into the light of day, I feel a wave of exhaustion wash over me. The weight of what we've faced is almost overwhelming, but there's a sense of accomplishment as well. We've faced the darkness and emerged victorious, and that's something to be proud of.

But the mansion still holds its secrets, and the shadows of the past will always linger. We've managed to stop the ritual, but there's still much to uncover, and the mansion's history is far from over.

Chapter 27

Ethan

The sun's rays pierce through the dense foliage surrounding the mansion, casting long shadows that stretch across the overgrown lawn. I feel a strange mixture of relief and trepidation as we step out of the mansion, its looming structure fading into the distance behind us. We've stopped the ritual, but the sense of finality is elusive. The mansion still holds many secrets, and I'm not convinced that the danger has entirely passed.

Maya, Jade, and I are silent as we walk away from the mansion, the weight of our recent ordeal heavy on our shoulders. The sunlight is a stark contrast to the oppressive darkness of the chamber we left behind, but the warmth does little to lift the chill that has settled within me.

"Are you okay?" Maya asks, glancing at me with concern. Her voice is soft, and I can see the fatigue etched on her face. The events of the past few days have taken their toll on all of us, and it's clear that we're all still processing what we've been through.

"I'm fine," I reply, though the words feel hollow. "Just... trying to wrap my head around everything."

Jade, who has been quiet for most of the walk, finally speaks up. "We need to figure out what to do next. The mansion is still out there, and we've only scratched the surface of its history. There might be more we need to uncover."

I nod in agreement. "You're right. There's still a lot we don't know. But for now, we need to rest and regroup. We can't keep pushing ourselves like this."

We head to the local diner, a familiar and comforting place where we can have a moment of normalcy. The smell of fresh coffee and baked goods fills the air, a welcome change from the musty, oppressive atmosphere of the mansion. As we sit down at a booth, the reality of what we've accomplished starts to settle in.

"So," Maya says, her eyes tired but determined. "What now? The ritual is stopped, but the mansion is still... there."

"I think we need to go back," I say, taking a sip of my coffee. "Not right away, but eventually. We need to understand more about the mansion's history and what really happened. There might be something we missed."

Jade nods in agreement. "We need to know what the mansion was hiding. It's clear that there's more to the story. And we need to make sure that whatever was awakened doesn't come back."

Maya looks thoughtful, her fingers tracing the rim of her coffee cup. "There's also the matter of the journal. It's filled with details about the ritual, but it didn't explain everything. There might be other documents or clues that could help us understand what we've faced."

As we discuss our plans, I can't help but feel a sense of unease. The mansion is no longer a distant, abstract threat; it's a tangible presence that has affected our lives in ways we can't fully comprehend. The ritual may be stopped, but the mansion's dark influence still lingers.

After we finish our meal, we head back to our homes, each of us needing some time to process everything. I arrive at my house, the familiar comfort of my room a stark contrast to the terror we faced. I sit down at my desk and pull out the journal from my bag, its pages filled with the remnants of our nightmare.

I flip through the pages, trying to piece together what we've learned. The symbols, the ritual, the watchers—it all feels like a jumble of incomprehensible fragments. But there's one thing that stands out: the mention of a hidden chamber beneath the mansion, a place where the ritual was almost completed.

I need to understand more about this hidden chamber. If there's something we missed, it could be crucial to fully ending the mansion's dark influence. I make a note to research any historical records or accounts of the mansion that might shed light on its secrets.

Later that night, I find myself unable to sleep, my mind racing with thoughts of the mansion and the ritual. I grab my laptop and start searching for any historical documents or local lore related to the mansion. It's a long shot, but I'm determined to uncover every detail.

As I dig through old newspaper articles and historical records, I come across an intriguing story. It's a newspaper article from the early 1900s, detailing a series of mysterious disappearances in the area surrounding the mansion. The disappearances were never solved, and the article mentions rumors of a secret society that may have been involved.

My heart races as I read through the article. The secret society could be connected to the ritual, and their involvement might explain some of the symbols and practices we've encountered. I make a note of the names and locations mentioned in the article, planning to investigate further.

I finally head to bed, the sense of unease still lingering. There's more to the mansion's story, and I'm determined to uncover it. The ritual may be stopped, but the shadows of the past still hold their secrets, and I'm ready to face whatever comes next.

Maya

The following morning, I wake up feeling drained but resolute. The weight of our recent experiences hangs heavily on me, and the need to uncover more about the mansion's dark history is a constant drive. As I get ready for the day, I can't shake the feeling that we've only scratched the surface of something much bigger.

I head to the local library, where Ethan and Jade are already waiting. We've decided to meet here to research more about the mansion and the mysterious secret society mentioned in the news-paper article. The library is a quiet refuge, a place where we can focus and dig into the history that might hold the answers we need.

Ethan is already at a table, his laptop open and a stack of old books spread out in front of him. Jade is beside him, flipping through a large volume of local history.

"Morning," I say as I sit down, joining them. "What have you found?"

Ethan looks up, his expression a mix of exhaustion and deter-mination. "I've been digging through local archives and historical records. There are a few references to the secret society mentioned in the article. They were known for their occult practices and had a reputation for secrecy."

Jade looks up from her book, her brow furrowed in concentration. "I found a few mentions of the society in old town records. They were linked to some of the more influential families in the area. It's possible that they were involved in the construction of the mansion."

I nod, my mind racing with the implications. "If the society was involved in the mansion's construction, they might have been the ones behind the ritual. We need to find out more about their practices and any records they left behind."

Ethan agrees, and we spend the next few hours poring over old records, newspaper articles, and historical accounts. The more we uncover, the clearer it becomes that the secret society was deeply involved in occult practices, and their influence extended throughout the region.

"We've got a few leads," Ethan says finally, looking up from his laptop. "There are records of their meetings and activities, and there's a mention of a hidden library where they kept their most valuable documents."

Jade's eyes widen. "A hidden library? That could be exactly what we need. If the society had a library, it might contain detailed records about their rituals and the mansion."

I feel a surge of hope at the thought. "We need to find this hidden library. It could hold the key to understanding everything."

We spend the rest of the day tracking down leads and following up on any clues related to the hidden library. It's a painstaking process, but we're determined to uncover the truth.

As the sun sets, we finally find a promising lead—a local historian who has done extensive research on the secret society. We arrange to meet with him the next day, hoping that he can provide us with more information about the hidden library and its location.

I head home that evening, feeling a mix of exhaustion and anticipation. We're one step closer to unraveling the mansion's secrets, and I can't wait to find out what lies ahead.

Chapter 28

Jade

The next morning, we head to the office of Dr. Andrew Collins, a local historian known for his extensive research on the area's dark past. The office is filled with dusty bookshelves, stacks of old newspapers, and various historical artifacts. The faint smell of old paper and ink lingers in the air, creating an atmosphere of solemnity and mystery.

Dr. Collins is an older man with a neatly trimmed beard and piercing gray eyes that seem to see right through you. He greets us warmly and invites us to sit down, his gaze shifting from each of us with keen interest.

"Thank you for coming," Dr. Collins says, his voice tinged with curiosity. "I understand you've uncovered some intriguing details about the old mansion and its connection to a secret society."

Ethan nods and pulls out the newspaper article we found, laying it on Dr. Collins's desk. "We discovered this article that mentions a series of mysterious disappearances linked to a secret society.

We believe this society was involved in occult practices and had a connection to the mansion."

Dr. Collins examines the article carefully, his brows furrowing as he reads through the details. "Yes, I've heard whispers of such a society. They were rumored to be involved in dark rituals and had a profound influence on the area. It's fascinating to see concrete evidence."

I lean in, my heart pounding with anticipation. "We also found references to a hidden library beneath the mansion. Do you have any information about its location or contents?"

Dr. Collins's eyes light up with recognition. "The hidden library—an intriguing piece of history. The society was known for its vast collection of occult texts and ritual tools, and the library was said to be a central part of their operations. It was rumored to be hidden beneath the mansion, accessible only through a series of secret passages."

I glance at Ethan, and he gives me a reassuring nod. "Do you know where we might find these secret passages? Any clues or maps that could guide us?"

Dr. Collins pulls out an old, faded map from a drawer and carefully unfolds it on his desk. The map is covered in intricate details, showing the layout of the mansion and the surrounding grounds. There are annotations in the margins, indicating various points of interest and potential hidden areas.

"This map," Dr. Collins explains, "dates back to the early 1900s and was part of the estate's original records. It shows the layout of the mansion and mentions several hidden passages. Some of these passages were rumored to lead to secret rooms, including the hidden library."

I study the map, my eyes tracing the lines and markings. "This is incredible. Do you have any idea where these passages might be located?"

Dr. Collins points to several areas on the map. "The passages are likely to be located in the mansion's less frequented areas. Look for concealed doors or hidden mechanisms—places that might not be obvious at first glance. The library was said to be located deep beneath the mansion, requiring several steps to reach."

Ethan nods thoughtfully. "We've already explored some of the mansion, but we might have missed these hidden areas. We'll need to go back and search carefully."

Dr. Collins leans back in his chair, his expression serious. "Be cautious. The society was known for its elaborate traps and protective measures. The hidden library won't be easy to access, and you might encounter obstacles designed to deter intruders."

Maya, who has been quietly listening, speaks up. "Thank you, Dr. Collins. This information is invaluable. We'll use the map and be careful as we search for the hidden library."

Dr. Collins nods, his eyes filled with a mix of concern and admiration. "I wish you luck. Uncovering the truth about the society and their activities is important, but it's also dangerous. Stay safe and be vigilant."

As we leave Dr. Collins's office, the weight of our next task feels more tangible. We have a map and a better understanding of what we're looking for, but the danger is far from over. The hidden library might hold the answers we need, but it will also test our resolve.

We head back to the mansion, the familiar sight of its imposing structure stirring a mix of apprehension and determination. The mansion looms over us, a dark and foreboding presence that seems to watch our every move. But we're more prepared now, armed with knowledge and a plan.

We enter the mansion through the back entrance, making our way to the areas we haven't explored yet. The map guides us as we search for concealed doors and hidden passages, our footsteps echoing in the eerie silence of the mansion.

Every creak of the floorboards and gust of wind through the old windows seems amplified in the stillness, heightening our sense of unease. We work methodically, checking every possible location and examining the walls for hidden mechanisms.

After several hours of searching, we finally discover a concealed door in the library—a door that was hidden behind a bookshelf and covered with dust. The door is old and weathered, its surface covered in intricate carvings that match the symbols we've seen before.

"This must be it," Ethan says, his voice filled with excitement and trepidation. "The entrance to the hidden library."

We push open the door, revealing a narrow staircase that descends into darkness. The air is cool and musty, carrying the faint scent of old books and forgotten secrets. We take a deep breath and begin our descent, the steps creaking beneath our weight.

As we make our way down the stairs, the darkness envelops us, and the anticipation builds with every step. We're about to uncover the secrets of the hidden library, and I can't help but feel a mixture of excitement and dread. What we find down here could change everything.

Chapter 29

E than

The narrow staircase descends deeper into the earth, the only source of light coming from the dim beam of our flashlight. Each step feels like a journey further from the world above, pulling us into the mansion's hidden depths. The air grows colder and denser, carrying a musty scent that speaks of centuries of neglect.

Maya, Jade, and I exchange nervous glances as we reach the bottom of the stairs. The passage opens into a large chamber, its walls lined with dusty shelves and old, rotting wooden beams. The hidden library, though covered in cobwebs and thick with age, exudes an undeniable sense of foreboding and intrigue.

"This is it," I whisper, my voice reverberating in the vast space. "The hidden library."

The room is dimly lit by the faint beam of our flashlights, revealing rows of shelves crammed with ancient books and artifacts. The air feels charged, as if the very atmosphere is holding its breath in anticipation of what we might find. The oppressive silence is broken only by the soft rustling of our movements and the occasional creak of the wooden floor.

Maya steps forward, her flashlight illuminating the spines of the books on the nearest shelf. "These look like they haven't been touched in years," she says, her voice filled with awe and a hint of fear. "There must be something important here."

Jade begins to sift through the books, carefully examining their covers and titles. "We need to find something that mentions the ritual or the society. The information could be hidden among these texts."

As we work, I notice a strange symbol etched into the floor near the center of the room. It's a complex design, reminiscent of the symbols we encountered during the ritual. My heart races as I realize that this symbol might be connected to the hidden passages or the secrets we're trying to uncover.

"Hey, check this out," I call to Maya and Jade, pointing to the symbol. "This looks like one of the symbols from the ritual."

Maya and Jade move over to examine the symbol. Maya crouches beside it, running her fingers over the etched lines. "It's definitely related to the ritual. I wonder if it's a key to something."

Jade studies the symbol with a thoughtful expression. "It could be a marker for a hidden mechanism or another passage. We should investigate further."

We carefully examine the area around the symbol, searching for any signs of a hidden mechanism or trap. After a few tense moments, Maya's flashlight reveals a small, concealed panel in the floor near the symbol. "I think we've found something."

With a collective effort, we pry open the panel, revealing a small compartment hidden beneath the floorboards. Inside, we find a leather-bound journal, its cover worn but intact. The journal is old and fragile, but it looks significant.

"This might be what we're looking for," Maya says, her voice filled with excitement. "Let's see what it says."

We open the journal and start to read through its pages. The handwriting is elegant but difficult to decipher, filled with descriptions of rituals, symbols, and the society's practices. As we turn the pages, we come across detailed accounts of the rituals performed in the mansion and the purpose behind them.

"This is incredible," I say, my voice filled with awe. "It's like a comprehensive record of everything the society did here."

Jade scans the pages, her expression focused. "There's a lot about the rituals, but there's also mention of something else—a hidden chamber that was intended to be used for the final phase of the ritual."

My heart skips a beat at the mention of the hidden chamber. "Do they say where it is?"

Jade continues reading, her eyes moving quickly over the text. "It looks like the hidden chamber is located deeper beneath the mansion. The journal describes a series of passages that lead to it, but it's not very specific about their locations."

Maya looks around the library, her eyes scanning the shelves. "We need to find these passages. If there's a final phase to the ritual, we have to make sure it's stopped completely."

We spend the next few hours searching the library for any additional clues or hidden passages. The process is painstaking, but our efforts eventually pay off. We discover another concealed door, partially obscured by a large, dusty bookshelf. The door leads to a narrow passage that descends even further into the earth.

"This must be the way to the hidden chamber," I say, feeling a surge of determination. "Let's go."

We navigate the narrow passage, our flashlights casting eerie shadows on the walls. The air grows colder and the space tighter, but we press on, driven by the need to uncover the truth and stop any lingering threats.

After what feels like an eternity, we reach the end of the passage. The hidden chamber is vast and imposing, filled with ancient symbols and ritualistic tools. In the center of the room stands an elaborate altar, covered in dust but still exuding an air of dark power.

"This is it," Maya says, her voice reverberating with a mix of awe and apprehension. "We've found the final phase of the ritual."

We carefully examine the altar and the surrounding area, looking for any signs of lingering danger or hidden traps. The chamber feels heavy with the remnants of dark magic, and I can't shake the feeling that we're not alone.

As we investigate, Jade spots a small, ornate box on a pedestal near the altar. "This could be important. Let's see what's inside."

We open the box to find a collection of ancient, intricately designed artifacts and a final set of instructions for the ritual. The instructions are detailed and elaborate, outlining the steps needed to complete the ritual and the consequences of its success.

"This is the key," I say, feeling a mixture of relief and dread. "With this, we can finally understand the full scope of the ritual and make sure it's completely stopped."

We carefully collect the artifacts and instructions, preparing to leave the hidden chamber. The sense of accomplishment is tempered by the lingering unease. The mansion's dark past has been revealed, but the true extent of its power and influence remains uncertain.

As we make our way back to the surface, the weight of what we've discovered settles heavily on our shoulders. The hidden chamber has provided us with crucial information, but the journey is far from over. We need to ensure that the ritual's influence is fully eradicated and that the mansion's dark legacy is put to rest.

We emerge from the mansion, the sunlight a stark contrast to the darkness we've left behind. The world above feels different now, and the shadows of the past still linger in our minds. But we've taken an important step toward uncovering the truth and stopping the darkness.

Chapter 30

Maya

The mansion looms before us, its dark silhouette casting long shadows in the late afternoon light. We've spent days preparing, deciphering the journal, and gathering everything we need for the final confrontation. The weight of what we've discovered hangs heavily in the air, mingling with the growing tension.

Ethan, Jade, and I stand in front of the mansion's entrance, our faces set with determination. The knowledge of the final phase of the ritual and the artifacts we've collected weigh heavily on our shoulders. This is it—the culmination of everything we've fought for.

"Are you ready?" Ethan asks, his voice steady but tinged with concern. His eyes meet mine, searching for reassurance.

I nod, trying to mask my own anxiety. "We have to be. We've come too far to back down now."

Jade checks the equipment one last time, her expression focused. "We need to be meticulous. The final chamber is the heart of the ritual, and it's likely to be heavily protected."

We push open the heavy doors of the mansion, the creaking sound echoing through the empty halls. The interior is as we left it—eerily quiet, with only the occasional sound of our footsteps breaking the silence. The sense of foreboding is palpable, but we press on, guided by the map and our determination.

The journey through the mansion feels different this time. The shadows seem darker, the silence more oppressive. Every creak of the floorboards and gust of wind through the old windows heightens our sense of unease.

We finally reach the hidden passage we discovered earlier, leading to the final chamber. The air grows colder as we descend, the passageway narrowing and twisting as if to test our resolve. We exchange glances, our resolve unshaken despite the growing tension.

As we reach the final chamber, the sight before us is both awe-inspiring and terrifying. The chamber is vast, with high ceilings and walls adorned with ancient symbols and dark rituals. The altar stands in the center, surrounded by a circle of flickering candles. The atmosphere is thick with the remnants of dark magic, and an oppressive silence fills the space.

"This is it," Ethan says, his voice barely above a whisper. "The heart of the ritual."

We cautiously enter the chamber, our footsteps echoing in the vast space. The artifacts we've collected are laid out on a nearby table, ready for use. We've prepared a counter-ritual to neutralize the dark magic and stop the final phase of the ritual.

Jade begins to set up the artifacts, carefully placing them according to the instructions in the journal. "We need to be precise. One mistake could undo everything."

Maya and I stand watch, our eyes scanning the chamber for any signs of danger. The silence is deafening, and the tension is almost unbearable. Every moment feels like a breath held in anticipation.

As Jade completes the setup, a low, rumbling sound echoes through the chamber. The candles flicker violently, casting eerie shadows on the walls. The temperature drops sharply, and a cold wind howls through the chamber.

"Something's happening," I say, my voice tinged with panic. "We need to act fast."

Jade nods, her expression grim. "Start the counter-ritual. We don't have much time."

We begin the ritual, reciting the incantations and performing the required actions with precision. The air crackles with energy, and the symbols on the walls seem to writhe and shift. The pressure in the room builds, and a sense of impending danger hangs over us.

As we work, a figure materializes at the edge of the chamber—a shadowy form with piercing eyes and an aura of malevolence. The figure moves with an otherworldly grace, its presence exuding a palpable sense of threat.

"It's the leader of the society," Ethan says, his voice filled with determination. "We have to finish the ritual before it's too late."

The figure advances toward us, its eyes glowing with an eerie light. The air becomes charged with dark energy, and the temperature drops further. The figure's gaze is fixed on us, and its presence feels suffocating.

"We're almost there," Jade says through gritted teeth. "Keep going."

The intensity of the moment is overwhelming. Our voices rise in unison as we recite the final incantations, the energy in the chamber reaching a crescendo. The dark figure howls in frustration, its form flickering and distorting as the ritual's power clashes with the counter-ritual.

The chamber is filled with a blinding light, and the air crackles with the force of the magic being unleashed. The dark figure's screams echo through the space, a sound of anguish and rage. The symbols on the walls glow brightly, their power reinforcing the counter-ritual.

With a final burst of energy, the chamber is filled with a deafening roar. The light intensifies, and the oppressive darkness is pushed back. The dark figure vanishes with a final, anguished cry, leaving the chamber in a profound silence.

Breathless and exhausted, we stand amidst the aftermath of the ritual. The air feels lighter, and the oppressive weight that has hung over us seems to have lifted. The chamber is still, and the candles have burned out, leaving us in the dim light of our flashlights.

"We did it," Ethan says, his voice filled with a mixture of relief and exhaustion. "The ritual is over."

Jade nods, her expression weary but satisfied. "We've neutralized the dark magic and stopped the final phase of the ritual. The society's influence should be gone for good."

Maya and I exchange a look, our faces reflecting the emotional weight of the moment. We've accomplished what we set out to do, but the journey has taken its toll. The mansion, once a place of fear and darkness, now feels like a silent witness to our victory.

As we make our way back to the surface, the sense of accomplishment is tempered by the exhaustion and the knowledge of what we've endured. The mansion's dark legacy has been confronted, but the echoes of its past will linger in our memories.

Chapter 31

Jade

The mansion stands behind us, its once-ominous presence now seemingly subdued by our victory. The night has fallen, casting a blanket of stars over the sky, a stark contrast to the darkness we've confronted. The air feels crisp and clear, as if the weight of the past has been lifted.

We gather in the garden outside the mansion, the cool evening air a welcome relief after the intense confrontation. The tension that has been building over the past weeks seems to dissipate, leaving behind a sense of weary satisfaction.

"Can you believe it's finally over?" Maya asks, her voice soft but filled with emotion. She gazes at the mansion, her eyes reflecting a mix of relief and lingering sadness.

I take a deep breath, trying to process the enormity of what we've just accomplished. "It's hard to believe. We've been through so much."

Ethan sits beside me, his face illuminated by the soft glow of the garden lights. "I didn't think we'd make it. There were times when it felt like the darkness would swallow us whole."

I nod in agreement. "But we did it. We faced the darkness head-on and stopped the ritual. The mansion's secrets are no longer a threat."

The silence that follows is filled with a sense of mutual understanding and reflection. We've accomplished something monumental, but the journey has left its mark on all of us. The emotional and physical toll of our ordeal is evident in our tired expressions and the quiet way we speak.

Maya breaks the silence, her voice tinged with gratitude. "I want to thank both of you. We couldn't have done this without each other. Your strength and determination made all the difference."

Ethan gives a tired smile. "We made a great team. I couldn't have asked for better allies in this fight."

We share a moment of camaraderie, the bond forged through our shared experiences and challenges. The trials we've faced have not only tested our courage but also brought us closer together.

As we sit together, the distant sound of sirens signals the arrival of the authorities. We've already contacted them about the mansion's dark history and the events that transpired. It's time to hand over the artifacts and the evidence we've gathered.

The authorities arrive, and we explain the situation, providing them with the journal, the artifacts, and our detailed account of what happened. They listen with a mix of skepticism and awe, clearly overwhelmed by the gravity of the situation.

"We'll take it from here," the lead officer says, his expression serious. "Thank you for your cooperation and for stopping whatever was going on here. This place has been a mystery for far too long."

We nod, knowing that our part in this story is coming to an end. The authorities will handle the aftermath, and the mansion's dark legacy will be dealt with by those equipped to handle it.

As we prepare to leave, Maya turns to us with a thoughtful expression. "What happens next for us? We've been so focused on the mansion and the ritual that we haven't really thought about the future."

Ethan looks at her with a hint of a smile. "We go back to our lives, I guess. But we've learned a lot about ourselves and each other through this experience. We're stronger because of it."

I agree, feeling a mixture of relief and uncertainty. "We've faced something extraordinary and come out the other side. Whatever happens next, we'll face it with the strength we've gained."

The night grows colder as we prepare to leave the mansion behind. The stars above seem to shine a little brighter, as if celebrating our victory. We share a final look at the mansion, knowing that our part in its story has come to an end.

As we walk away from the mansion, the sense of closure begins to settle in. The darkness that once threatened us has been confronted and vanquished. We've done what we set out to do, and the world feels a little bit lighter for it.

The road ahead is uncertain, but we're ready to face it. The challenges we've overcome have prepared us for whatever comes next. We're leaving behind a chapter filled with darkness, but we're stepping into a future filled with hope and possibility.

Maya

The mansion now sits silent and empty, a relic of a dark chapter in our lives. The authorities have taken over, ensuring that any remnants of the ritual and the society's influence are thoroughly investigated and dealt with. The weight of what we've accomplished is starting to settle, and the world feels oddly calm in comparison to the chaos we've just been through.

Ethan, Jade, and I have gathered at a small café in town. It's our first day back to something resembling normalcy. The warmth and light inside are a stark contrast to the cold, oppressive atmosphere of the mansion. We sit around a table, each of us nursing a cup of coffee or tea, trying to process the recent events.

"This feels surreal," Ethan says, stirring his coffee absently. "Like we've stepped out of a nightmare and into a dream."

Jade nods, her eyes distant. "It's hard to believe it's all over. We went through so much, and now it's like we're waking up from a long, intense dream."

Maya looks around the café, her expression contemplative. "I'm relieved it's over, but I keep thinking about everything we lost along the way. Lena's story, the people affected by the society's actions..."

"It's a lot to process," I say, my voice filled with a mixture of sadness and acceptance. "But we did what we could. We stopped the ritual and brought the truth to light. That's something to hold onto."

The conversation drifts to more personal matters as we each share our thoughts and feelings about the journey. The shared experiences have created a strong bond between us, and we find comfort in each other's company.

Maya breaks the silence, her voice soft but determined. "We've been through so much together. I think it's important that we take the time to heal and figure out what comes next for us."

Ethan looks at Maya with a thoughtful expression. "You're right. We've been so focused on the mission that we haven't really thought about our own futures. What do we want to do now?"

Jade's eyes light up with a hint of excitement. "Maybe this is our chance to start fresh. We've faced something extraordinary, and it's changed us. Perhaps it's time to embrace those changes and see where they lead us."

The conversation shifts to our plans and dreams for the future. We discuss the possibilities with a sense of hope and optimism, despite the challenges we've faced. The experience has given us a new perspective on life, and we're ready to embrace whatever comes next.

As the afternoon wears on, the café fills with the sounds of laughter and conversation from other patrons. The normalcy of it all is comforting, and we allow ourselves to enjoy the moment of peace and tranquility.

Later that day, we take a walk through the park, the crisp air and vibrant colors of the fall leaves offering a welcome change from the dark confines of the mansion. We talk about our dreams and aspirations, sharing our hopes for the future and the changes we want to make in our lives.

"I've been thinking about going back to school," Maya says, her voice filled with determination. "I want to study psychology and help people who've gone through traumatic experiences."

Ethan nods in agreement. "That sounds like a great idea. I've been considering pursuing a career in investigative journalism. I want to continue uncovering the truth and making a difference."

Jade smiles, her eyes sparkling with excitement. "I've always wanted to explore the world and experience different cultures. I think now is the perfect time to travel and find out what I really want to do."

We share our plans with a sense of excitement and anticipation. The future feels bright and full of possibilities, and we're eager to see where our new paths will lead us.

As the sun sets, casting a warm glow over the park, we pause to take in the beauty of the moment. The challenges we've faced have strengthened our resolve and given us a deeper appreciation for the world around us.

The journey has been long and arduous, but it has also been transformative. We've faced our fears, confronted the darkness, and emerged stronger and more connected. The mansion's shadows have been left behind, and we're ready to step into the future with hope and determination.

As we part ways at the end of the day, there's a sense of closure and renewal. The story of the mansion and its dark legacy is behind us, but the lessons we've learned and the bonds we've forged will remain with us.

We've faced the darkness and come out stronger on the other side. Now, as we step into our new beginnings, we carry with us the strength and resilience that have defined our journey.

Chapter 32

Maya

The mansion now sits silent and empty, a relic of a dark chapter in our lives. The authorities have taken over, ensuring that any remnants of the ritual and the society's influence are thoroughly investigated and dealt with. The weight of what we've accomplished is starting to settle, and the world feels oddly calm in comparison to the chaos we've just been through.

Ethan, Jade, and I have gathered at a small café in town. It's our first day back to something resembling normalcy. The warmth and light inside are a stark contrast to the cold, oppressive atmosphere of the mansion. We sit around a table, each of us nursing a cup of coffee or tea, trying to process the recent events.

"This feels surreal," Ethan says, stirring his coffee absently. "Like we've stepped out of a nightmare and into a dream."

Jade nods, her eyes distant. "It's hard to believe it's all over. We went through so much, and now it's like we're waking up from a long, intense dream."

Maya looks around the café, her expression contemplative. "I'm relieved it's over, but I keep thinking about everything we lost along the way. Lena's story, the people affected by the society's actions..."

"It's a lot to process," I say, my voice filled with a mixture of sadness and acceptance. "But we did what we could. We stopped the ritual and brought the truth to light. That's something to hold onto."

The conversation drifts to more personal matters as we each share our thoughts and feelings about the journey. The shared experiences have created a strong bond between us, and we find comfort in each other's company.

Maya breaks the silence, her voice soft but determined. "We've been through so much together. I think it's important that we take the time to heal and figure out what comes next for us."

Ethan looks at Maya with a thoughtful expression. "You're right. We've been so focused on the mission that we haven't really thought about our own futures. What do we want to do now?"

Jade's eyes light up with a hint of excitement. "Maybe this is our chance to start fresh. We've faced something extraordinary, and it's changed us. Perhaps it's time to embrace those changes and see where they lead us."

The conversation shifts to our plans and dreams for the future. We discuss the possibilities with a sense of hope and optimism, despite the challenges we've faced. The experience has given us a new perspective on life, and we're ready to embrace whatever comes next.

As the afternoon wears on, the café fills with the sounds of laughter and conversation from other patrons. The normalcy of it all is comforting, and we allow ourselves to enjoy the moment of peace and tranquility.

Later that day, we take a walk through the park, the crisp air and vibrant colors of the fall leaves offering a welcome change from the dark confines of the mansion. We talk about our dreams and aspirations, sharing our hopes for the future and the changes we want to make in our lives.

"I've been thinking about going back to school," Maya says, her voice filled with determination. "I want to study psychology and help people who've gone through traumatic experiences."

Ethan nods in agreement. "That sounds like a great idea. I've been considering pursuing a career in investigative journalism. I want to continue uncovering the truth and making a difference."

Jade smiles, her eyes sparkling with excitement. "I've always wanted to explore the world and experience different cultures. I think now is the perfect time to travel and find out what I really want to do."

We share our plans with a sense of excitement and anticipation. The future feels bright and full of possibilities, and we're eager to see where our new paths will lead us.

As the sun sets, casting a warm glow over the park, we pause to take in the beauty of the moment. The challenges we've faced have strengthened our resolve and given us a deeper appreciation for the world around us.

The journey has been long and arduous, but it has also been transformative. We've faced our fears, confronted the darkness, and emerged stronger and more connected. The mansion's shadows have been left behind, and we're ready to step into the future with hope and determination.

As we part ways at the end of the day, there's a sense of closure and renewal. The story of the mansion and its dark legacy is behind us, but the lessons we've learned and the bonds we've forged will remain with us.

We've faced the darkness and come out stronger on the other side. Now, as we step into our new beginnings, we carry with us the strength and resilience that have defined our journey.

Chapter 33

E than

The weeks have slipped by in a blur of activity and adjustment. With the mansion's dark influence removed, the town seems to be slowly returning to normal, though the echoes of our ordeal linger in our minds. We've settled into new routines, and each of us is trying to piece together a semblance of normal life after the whirlwind of our recent experiences.

Today, I find myself standing on the porch of my small apartment, looking out at the busy street below. The familiar sights of the town are comforting, a reminder of the ordinary life that once felt so distant. I'm trying to sort through my thoughts and feelings, but it's a struggle to reconcile the calm with the chaos we faced.

My phone buzzes with a text from Maya: *"Meeting at the park later? We need to talk about our next steps."* I text back my agreement and make my way to the park, hoping that our conversation will help us all make sense of our experiences and what lies ahead.

When I arrive at the park, the familiar surroundings bring a sense of nostalgia. The park was one of our frequent hangouts before everything changed, and it feels strangely comforting to be here again. I spot Maya and Jade already seated at a bench, deep in conversation.

"Hey," I greet them as I approach, trying to sound more upbeat than I feel. "How's it going?"

Maya looks up with a smile. "Hey, Ethan. We were just discussing what we should do next. We've been so focused on recovering and adjusting that we haven't really talked about our future."

Jade nods in agreement. "It's time to start thinking about what comes next. We've been through so much together, and it's important that we set new goals and move forward."

We take a seat on the bench, the warm sunlight filtering through the leaves of the trees above. The park is bustling with people enjoying the pleasant weather, a stark contrast to the dark atmosphere of the mansion.

"I've been doing a lot of thinking," I start, my voice thoughtful. "The experience has changed me in ways I didn't expect. I'm considering pursuing a career in investigative journalism, like I mentioned before. I want to continue uncovering truths and helping people understand the world around them."

Maya's eyes light up. "That sounds like a great plan. Your passion for finding the truth is evident, and I think it's a path you'll excel in."

Jade adds, "I think it's important that we follow our passions and make the most of the new perspectives we've gained. I'm still planning to travel and explore different cultures. There's so much to see and learn, and I want to embrace every opportunity."

Maya takes a deep breath and looks at us with a serious expression. "There's something else I've been thinking about. The experience we went through was incredibly intense, and it's left a mark on all of us. I want to use my experiences to help others who have gone through trauma. I'm considering going back to school to study psychology and become a therapist."

"That's a powerful choice," I say, nodding in agreement. "You have the empathy and understanding that can really make a difference in people's lives."

As we continue our conversation, the park around us seems to fade into the background. We're focused on the future and the new paths we're each charting. The weight of our past experiences is still present, but we're determined to move forward with purpose and hope.

We spend the rest of the afternoon discussing our plans in detail, each of us sharing our aspirations and dreams. The conversation is filled with a mixture of excitement and apprehension, as we acknowledge the challenges ahead while embracing the opportunities.

The sun begins to set, casting a warm glow over the park. The sky is painted in shades of orange and pink, and the cool evening air feels refreshing. We reluctantly rise from the bench, our conversation having given us a sense of clarity and direction.

"I'm glad we had this talk," Maya says, her voice filled with gratitude. "It feels good to share our plans and support each other as we move forward."

"Definitely," Jade agrees. "We've been through so much together, and I think it's important that we continue to be there for each other."

As we part ways, there's a sense of closure and anticipation. The park, once a backdrop for our past gatherings, now feels like a symbol of our new beginning. We've faced the darkness and emerged stronger, and we're ready to embrace the future with hope and determination.

Walking home, I reflect on the journey we've undertaken and the changes it has brought. The experiences we've shared have shaped us in profound ways, and while the scars of the past may never fully fade, they have also given us strength and resilience.

The world outside feels different now, but in a way that's invigorating rather than frightening. We've confronted the darkness and come out on the other side, and now it's time to build a new chapter in our lives.

I arrive back at my apartment, feeling a sense of calm and purpose. The future is uncertain, but I'm ready to face it with the knowledge that we've overcome extraordinary challenges and emerged as stronger individuals.

As I settle into my evening routine, I'm filled with a renewed sense of hope and determination. The journey is far from over, but the path ahead is now clear. We've faced the darkness, and now we're ready to embrace the light.

Epilogue

J ade

The sun is barely up when I find myself standing in front of the old mansion one last time. The town has been quick to shut it down, sealing off the grounds with bright yellow caution tape, as if that could keep out the memories that haunt this place. The windows, once darkened and grimy, now stare blankly back at me, as if the house itself has been emptied of whatever malevolent force once thrived within its walls.

Yet, despite the quiet, I can't help but feel that the mansion still holds something—an echo, a remnant of all that transpired here. It's a feeling that's been gnawing at me ever since we walked out of this place. I thought I'd feel relief, but all I can sense is this unfinished business, something I haven't been able to shake.

I take a deep breath and step closer to the building. The air is cold, almost unnaturally so for this time of year, and it prickles my skin, raising goosebumps on my arms. There's a part of me that knows I shouldn't be here, that we've done what we came to do, and it's time to move on. But there's another part that can't let go—not until I'm sure there's nothing left to be found.

"Jade?" Maya's voice cuts through my thoughts, pulling me back to the present. I turn to see her standing at the gate, looking as if she's been following me, tracking my every step. She's bundled up against the chill, her face a mix of concern and understanding.

"Maya," I say, forcing a smile. "I didn't think you'd be here."

She walks over to me, her eyes never leaving mine. "I could say the same about you. I had a feeling you'd come back."

I nod, trying to find the right words to explain why I'm here, but everything feels inadequate. "I don't know, Maya. I just—there's something about this place. It doesn't feel over."

She studies me for a moment, then glances at the mansion. "You think there's still something inside?"

"I don't know," I admit. "Maybe it's just my mind playing tricks on me, but I can't shake the feeling that we missed something—something important."

Maya doesn't respond right away. Instead, she steps closer to the mansion, her eyes scanning the building as if she, too, is searching for answers. "You're not the only one who feels that way," she finally says. "I've been having these weird dreams, ever since we left. It's like the mansion's trying to tell me something."

I blink, surprised. Maya's always been the most level-headed of us, the one who could keep her cool even when everything else was falling apart. If she's feeling this way too, then maybe I'm not as crazy as I thought.

"What kind of dreams?" I ask.

Maya shrugs, but her eyes are distant, like she's recalling something that both intrigues and unsettles her. "It's hard to explain. It's always the same—I'm standing in the mansion, but it's different. The walls are covered in these strange symbols, and there's this... presence. I can't see it, but I know it's there, watching me. It feels like it's waiting for something."

Her words send a shiver down my spine, and I pull my jacket tighter around me. "Do you think it means something? That we should go back in?"

Maya hesitates, and for a moment, I think she's going to say no. But then she looks me in the eye, and I see the determination there, the same determination that got us through this whole ordeal. "I think we have to," she says softly. "If there's even a chance that something was left unfinished, we can't ignore it. Not after everything we've been through."

I nod, feeling that same resolve harden within me. We're not just doing this for ourselves—we're doing it for everyone who's been affected by the mansion's dark history. For everyone who never got the chance to walk away.

Together, we make our way to the front door. It's still slightly ajar, just as we left it, and with a gentle push, it creaks open, revealing the dim, dusty interior. The smell of decay and age hits me immediately, and for a moment, I'm overwhelmed by the memories—the terror, the pain, the loss.

But I push through it, stepping inside with Maya right behind me. The air is heavy, thick with an oppressive silence that feels almost alive. Every footstep echoes through the empty halls, and as we make our way deeper into the mansion, that feeling of being watched only grows stronger.

We pass through the familiar rooms, the grand staircase, the endless corridors. It all looks the same, and yet there's a new tension in the air, a sense that something is different—something we can't quite place.

We finally reach the heart of the mansion, the room where everything came to a head. The ritual chamber. The place where we faced down the darkness and won—or so we thought.

The room is as we left it—bare, with only the faintest traces of the symbols that once lined the walls. But there's a coldness here that wasn't there before, a feeling that makes the hairs on the back of my neck stand up.

Maya steps forward, her eyes scanning the room with a sharp intensity. "It's here," she whispers. "Whatever it is, it's still here."

I don't doubt her. The air feels thick with tension, and there's an undercurrent of something... wrong. Like a hum that you can't hear, but can feel deep in your bones.

"We need to figure out what it wants," I say, my voice hushed. "Why it's still here."

Maya nods, and together, we begin searching the room, looking for anything out of place, any sign that might tell us what we're dealing with. It doesn't take long before Maya's hand brushes against something on the floor, and she kneels down to get a closer look.

"It's a carving," she says, tracing the outline with her fingers. "It wasn't here before."

I kneel beside her, staring at the intricate symbol etched into the wood. It's like nothing I've ever seen before, a swirling design that seems to twist and turn in on itself, drawing the eye deeper and deeper into its center.

"Do you think it's part of the ritual?" I ask, feeling a cold dread settle in my stomach.

Maya shakes her head. "No. This is something else. I think... I think it's a warning."

"A warning?" I echo, my voice barely above a whisper.

"Yeah," Maya says, her voice tense. "I think whoever—or what-ever—left this is trying to tell us that it's not over. That there's still something here, something dangerous."

The words hang in the air, heavy with implication. My mind races, trying to piece together what this could mean. If the ritual isn't over, if there's still something here, then we're not done. We're not safe.

"We need to leave," I say, standing up quickly. "We need to get out of here and figure out what this means. We can't stay."

But as I turn to leave, a cold gust of wind rushes through the room, slamming the door shut with a deafening bang. The temperature drops sharply, and the lights flicker, plunging us into near darkness.

Maya grabs my arm, her grip tight with fear. "Jade..."

I can feel it too—a presence, something dark and powerful, press-ing down on us from all sides. The air is thick with it, making it hard to breathe, hard to think.

"We have to go," I say, my voice shaking. "Now!"

But the door won't budge. No matter how hard we push or pull, it stays firmly shut, trapping us inside.

Panic starts to claw at the edges of my mind, but I force it down, focusing on finding another way out. There has to be some-thing—some way to escape before whatever is in this room decides to show itself.

But then, just as suddenly as it started, the presence begins to fade. The temperature rises, the lights stabilize, and the door creaks open as if it had never been stuck at all.

Maya and I exchange a look, both of us breathing hard, our hearts pounding in our chests.

"What was that?" she asks, her voice trembling.

"I don't know," I reply, equally shaken. "But whatever it was, it's gone now. At least for the moment."

We don't need to be told twice. We leave the room as quickly as we can, making our way back through the mansion, our nerves on high alert for any sign of danger.

When we finally step outside into the cool morning air, it feels like a weight has been lifted off our shoulders. The mansion looms behind us, silent and still, but the memory of what just happened is fresh in our minds.

"I think we were right," Maya says, her voice quiet. "It's not over. Whatever we faced before—it's still here, and it's not going to let go easily."

I nod, my mind racing with thoughts of what this could mean. "We need to find out more about this symbol, this presence. We can't just walk away and hope it goes away on its own."

Maya agrees. "We'll have to dig deeper, find out the truth about this place. There's something here that we don't understand, and if we don't figure it out, it's going to keep coming back."

There's a resolve in her voice that matches the determination I feel. We've been through too much to walk away now. If the mansion still holds secrets, we're going to uncover them—no matter what it takes.

As we leave the mansion behind, I can't help but glance back one last time. The morning light casts long shadows across the lawn, and for a moment, I think I see a figure standing in one of the windows, watching us. But when I blink, it's gone, leaving me wondering if it was just a trick of the light—or something more.

Whatever the case, one thing is certain: this isn't the end. The mansion has more to tell us, and we're not leaving until we've heard every last word.

www.ingramcontent.com/pod-product-compliance
Lightning Source LLC
Chambersburg PA
CBHW070956180726
48291CB00004B/1309